THE
FATAL
FLAW

THE
FATAL
FLAW

LAURENCE MEYNELL

A JUBILEE MYSTERY
STEIN AND DAY/*Publishers*/New York

First published in the United States of America, 1978
Copyright © 1973 by Laurence Meynell
All rights reserved
Printed in the United States of America
Stein and Day/*Publishers*/Scarborough House
Briarcliff Manor, N.Y. 10510

Library of Congress Cataloging in Publication Data

Meynell, Laurence Walter, 1899–
The fatal flaw.

I.   Title.
[PZ3.M5774Fat   1977]   [PR6025.E93]   823'.9'12
ISBN 0-8128-2419-9   77-17997

I

Detective Inspector William Lawson could not possibly have known it but the problem he found himself confronted with in Amminster really had its roots in a meeting seven months before in a flat in St John's Wood, London.

The ground-floor flat of a tall, well-built, well-appointed house.

Not a cheap flat by any means, and one much liked and well looked after by the two men who shared it.

Being on the ground floor the flat had access to the patch of garden at the back of the house, but neither Gerald Marston nor Philip Manderville availed themselves much of this amenity.

Manderville thought flowers were 'marvellous' (a great word with him, this sadly overworked 'marvellous') but he knew nothing about them and regarded gardening, as he regarded practically all activities outside his own enclosed world of the theatre, as something slightly unreal and beyond comprehension.

Marston, the barrister, was busy nearly every evening during the week with papers which he brought back from his Chambers in the Temple and at week-ends he usually managed to secure an invitation to the country. Like all true Londoners he considered trees and grass as untidy interruptions in the orderly layout of pavement and street.

Both men were young – Gerald Marston was no more than twenty-seven, Philip Manderville was thirty-one – and in the climate of today's outlook it was inevitable that a certain number of their friends should assume that they were homosexuals, living together.

In fact this wasn't so. Marston was rather strongly

heterosexual; Manderville, like many actors, not particularly one thing or the other.

Sharing the flat had been a matter of finance only.

Marston, who had an eye for an elegant house, had suddenly been given the chance of taking the flat on a longish lease and found himself simultaneously unable to say 'no', because he liked the flat so much; and equally unable to say 'yes', because the rent asked was beyond him.

At precisely this juncture he went to a part-legal, part-medical, part-theatrical party and met Philip Manderville, then appearing in an over-dressed, pseudo-Tudor series on television.

The talk turning on houses, flats, prices, rents and accommodation generally, it emerged that Manderville had to leave wherever he was at the moment and was looking for somewhere to live. The two men had taken a liking to one another and there and then struck a bargain. The rent was halved, the accommodation was halved and both found it an admirable arrangement.

It was, in fact, neither Gerald Marston, the rising young barrister, nor Philip Manderville, the never-to-be-a-star-but-never-the-less-constantly-employed actor, who was directly responsible for the subsequent trouble in Amminster – unless, indeed, you blame Manderville because it was he who brought the visitor to the flat that evening.

Vyvyan Weighman.

Thin and dark this Vyvyan Weighman; his dress carefully casual in the modern manner; very much a man of his time and generation.

Marston had stayed in all the evening, hedged about by the usual set of papers; Manderville had gone to a buffet party given by an adoring and wealthy woman to call the attention of the world to the merits of a novel written by her daughter and published that very day.

'Marvellous, Dorothy darling,' everybody said, picking up the displayed copy of the newly born novel from its

6

place hard by the champagne bottles, examining its some-what flamboyant jacket and carefully putting it down again. 'I simply don't know how you do it.'

Philip Manderville went through the prescribed routine and the thin, dark man standing just behind him and watching the performance with a slightly sardonic air, asked, 'Ever read any of her others?'

'I don't think I have, actually,' Philip had to confess. 'Are they any good?'

A thin smile and 'You mustn't ask me. We are doing the publicity for her.'

'You are in the publicity world?'

'Taylor, Mason & Fitzwarren.'

Manderville already felt intrigued by this man with the quiet voice who somehow gave the impression of having depth to him; a good deal in reserve.

'Taylor? Mason? or Fitzwarren?' Manderville asked.

'Nothing so exalted. Employed by them only. Vyvyan Weighman – with an e-i-g-h. I know you, of course —'

I know you, of course – sweet music to any actor's ear; Manderville smiled and did his best to look modest.

'I've seen you on the box in that historical series. Quite honestly I don't think much of the series, but you were good.'

Manderville was by now convinced that his new companion was not only a good fellow but also an extremely perceptive critic, and during the evening the two men – each having come to the party on his own – tended to keep together.

When it looked as though the champagne might be beginning to run out and when the supply of overworked superlatives about the newly published book was exhausted people started to fade away.

'Which direction are you going in?' Weighman asked.

'Regent's Park. Any use to you? Can we share a cab, perhaps?'

'No need. I've got a car. I'll give you a lift.'

On the way to Regent's Park Weighman asked, 'What happens when we get there? A house; or flat; or what?'

'Half a flat to be precise. I share with another man. A barrister, Gerald Marston. A really brainy character. Everyone says he's sure to take silk before long. You must come in and have a drink. You'll like him.'

But it didn't work out that way.

Manderville seldom gave a thought to the unreal world outside the theatre; when he did think about it at all he was perpetually dismayed by the failure of people to get on with one another. Wrapped up in the cocoon of intense jealousies, envies, hopes and despairs of his chosen world he was genuinely shocked to find that the larger world outside wasn't perpetually flowing with the milk and honey of kindness and understanding. *Why can't everybody be friends?* he was always asking himself.

Gerald Marston, the rising young barrister so evidently destined to take silk before long, could be a little pompous at times and it quickly became evident that the visitor didn't like pomposity.

Because of the champagne nature of the earlier part of the evening Weighman opted for brandy when asked what he would like to drink. Manderville joined him, and after a certain amount of deliberation and knowledgeable chatter ('straight out of the Good Food Guide' Weighman thought) Gerald Marston decided to open half a bottle of claret for himself.

Weighman listened to the preliminary *spiel* and watched the uncorking, bouquet-sampling, pouring out, tasting and (inevitably) approving with sardonic amusement.

'Weighman's in publicity,' Manderville said.

'Really?'

'Taylor, Mason & Fitzwarren.'

'I think I've heard of them.'

Pompous bastard, Weighman thought, just like these

legal types. He himself didn't care much for Taylor; thought Mason was a fraud; and positively hated Fitzwarren's guts; but everybody at least knew of the firm. This 'I think I've heard of them' affectation was too patronising to be borne.

'You follow the law, don't you?' he asked.

'I'm a barrister.'

'Weren't you in this hold-up and robbery case just finished at the Old Bailey?'

'I was. Sir Mathew Antrim led and I was his junior.'

'I thought the poor sod was unlucky to be convicted.'

'Unlucky? Why? He was guilty.'

'You legal types said so. But how often does truth get distorted in a court of law?'

'You're not suggesting that the courts are crooked, are you?'

'When a man sticks a wig on his head, and puts on a red robe and gets called "Judge" by everybody in reverential tones he frequently confuses himself with God. I think that's a mistake. And anyway I merely said the fellow was unlucky. Perhaps I should have said silly. If he had taken just a little more trouble in thinking out the job I don't see why he should have been caught, let alone found guilty.'

'I think you rather over-estimate the intelligence of the criminal. It's a tendency people have who read the more sensational Sunday papers.'

Philip Manderville sighed and took a sip at his brandy. He was now beginning to regret having brought this, to him, pleasant new acquaintance in for a drink.

But to his relief there were no real fireworks. Weighman swirling his brandy round in the balloon glass simply said quietly, even somewhat meekly, 'Maybe.'

'The Law isn't stupid, you know.'

'You could have fooled me.'

'It's the criminal who's stupid. Ask any policeman. Maybe you don't have to deal with the police much in

Taylor, whatever-it-is & Fitzthing. But I do. A barrister who handles criminal cases sees a lot of the police. Any policeman will tell you that the man who commits a crime always makes a mistake.'

'I don't see why he should. If one gave sufficient thought and preparation to it; took enough trouble; it would be perfectly possible to plan a hold-up which was foolproof.'

'That mythical thing – the perfect crime.'

'Why not?'

'I wouldn't advise you to try it.'

'I didn't say I was going to try to do it, I merely said it could be done; of course' – Weighman suddenly smiled his thin, dark smile – '*foolproof* is a relative term. A man I know who was in the R.A.F. in the war has a good tale about that. A Flight-Sergeant was showing him some gadget or other which was designed to make for safety.

' "That's all right, Flight," the man said when the thing had been explained to him, "but is it foolproof?"

'The Flight-Sergeant considered for a moment and then replied cautiously, "Well, sir, it's foolproof, but it isn't bloody foolproof."

'Rather a nice distinction I thought.'

Manderville laughed heartily, glad of anything which would ease the tension that had undoubtedly sprung up between the other two men.

When Weighman had left ('I'm living over in the Chelsea direction,' he told them vaguely) Manderville said, 'I'm sorry about that. He and I got on quite well at the party, but bringing him back here wasn't much of a success, was it?'

'I don't care for his type. In fact I don't care for *him*. You know who he is I suppose?'

'I've no idea. I've never met him before in my life. Do you know him, then?'

'I know of him.'

'You're an extraordinary man, Gerald; you seem to know

everybody.'

'The Law is funny that way. It's just about the tightest enclave (Trades Union our enemies call it) in the world, yet in it one does tend to come in contact with all sorts of people, living in all sorts of conditions.'

'And Vyvyan Weighman?'

'People come to the law, you see, either when they are angry or when they are in trouble; and in both cases one generally sees the worst side of them. Vyvyan Weighman is the son of Sir Lucian Weighman who figured (the papers came through our Chambers actually) in a rather unpleasant divorce case. That was his first wife – the mother of the man who was here this evening. Father and son fell out over the second wife; I don't imagine they were ever particularly *sympatica*; and they said some pretty nasty things about one another both in print and goaded on by those damned interviewers on radio and TV.'

'And what sort is Sir Lucian – the grand old English gentleman type?'

'With qualifications; that is to say, his grandfather was probably a Jewish tailor in Hamburg; at a guess his father came to the East End of Victorian London with less than five pounds in his pocket and ended up in Belgravia with a great great deal of money.

'Money which Lucian used very sensibly; he bought a title, married a minor aristocrat, sent his son to Eton and of all unlikely things set the seal on his achievements by becoming President of the M.C.C. – as you justly remark, a fine old English gentleman.'

'But no love lost between him and Vyvyan?'

'None at all I should say. To some extent my sympathies are with the old man. You don't read the papers much do you?'

'The theatre columns.'

'Vyvyan Weighman has got himself into the news once or twice; never, one imagines, in a way that would please his father. There was that musical group he was concerned with, for instance, called "The Navels" which involved him in a lot of notoriety, and then there was the rough-house at the Confrontation night club.'

'Is he married?' Manderville asked.

'I've no idea. But I should think it extremely probable. He's the type of man who will always manage to have some woman besotted about him.'

II

It wouldn't be correct to say that Barbara Courlander was besotted about Vyvyan.

She was too strong-willed, too much of a person in her own right, for that to be true.

They were living together because of a very strong physical attraction between them and – at least an equal reason – because they both shared the same outlook on life: there is a glorious lot of money about in the world, let's grab all we can; there is a depressing lot of misery about, let's avoid it as much as possible; there's a splendid lot of restlessness, movement and noise, let's never be without it. It was the modern blueprint for living, and neither of them saw a valid alternative anywhere.

Barbara had not gone to the novel-launching jamboree partly because of a slight sore throat, but mostly because she loathed the woman novelist in question. Women novelists in general were one of her pet hates ('*Christ, these Ednas and Margarets and Elizabeths, how does anyone manage to be so boring?*').

The morning after the novel-launching Barbara sat opposite Vyvyan at the breakfast table holding her cup of coffee between her strong, capable hands.

They were sitting in a tiny recess in the intensely modern kitchen of a flat in Hambledon Street off the King's Road, Chelsea.

Barbara didn't expect the account of the party to be particularly interesting and she only half listened to it '... lots of people of course; well, with free champers you would expect it, wouldn't you? Nobody particularly interesting. Dorothy's fond mamma ramming the book down everyone's throat. With the most ghastly jacket you ever saw in your life. Why don't they get somebody decent to design these things?'

'Anyone we know there?'

'Two or three; but —' Vyvyan shook his head. For him and Barbara their acquaintances were divided into 'beings' and 'non-beings'; the shake of his head meant that the two or three people he had known at the party were of the non-being variety.

'I chummed up with Philip Manderville.'

'The actor?' Barbara was slightly more interested. 'Did you tell him what we think about that mock-Tudor nonsense on the box?'

'I didn't perjure myself. I told him I thought he personally was good. Which I do.'

Barbara grimaced.

'Well, fair anyway. But you can't tell an actor you think he's "fair" so I said "good". Which, of course, opened the way to his heart and when I told him I could provide transport he asked me back to his flat for a drink.'

'Where?'

'Regent's Park. He shares with a lawyer type. Barrister, actually. Gerald somebody – Marston, I think.'

'Are they living together? Homos?'

'Could be. I didn't ask. If they are I can't congratulate Manderville on his choice; Marston's a pompous sort of bastard.'

'What did you talk about?'

'Oh, I don't know. Nothing much. The perfect crime.'

'The perfect crime?'

'I forget how it came up. Marston said the Law always wins; the Mountie always gets his man. Just to annoy him I said "Why?" If a villain gave enough thought to it and took enough trouble he doesn't have to make the one traditional mistake.'

'You're probably right,' Barbara agreed. 'You must try it

14

some time. Meanwhile what about T.M. & F.? Are they going to give you a lot more lovely money?'

'It's a question of renewing my contract with them. I've got to see Toni Fitzwarren today about it.'

'He's the one you don't like, isn't he?'

'Can't stand the supercilious sod.'

'All the same I wouldn't actually throw things at him. What you want is a longer contract on better terms.'

'Very neatly put, Bar.'

Barbara went to the hot-plate, poured herself out a second cup of coffee and lit a cigarette.

When she sat down again she went on, 'I suppose that horrible old father of yours will die some time and then there'll be no problem; but meanwhile the more money you can screw out of T.M. & F. the better, darling.'

'I couldn't agree more,' Vyvyan said.

Toni Fitzwarren somewhat wearily pushed to one side a sheaf of sketches of plump-faced, chocolate-sucking children. Somehow the artist hadn't got them quite right ... not plump enough? Not sucking hard enough? Fitzwarren couldn't make up his mind what was wrong exactly; meanwhile he had other things, one other thing in particular, to deal with.

He asked his twenty-three-year-old secretary to take the sketches away, and watched with approval her strong white thighs under the miniest of mini-skirts as she did so.

He pressed a button on the intercom and lowering his head slightly towards the instrument said, 'Arnold, can you come in for a minute.'

Arnold Mason came in from his own office next door, a plump, soft, white old man of not yet forty.

Mason might be plump, soft and white and prematurely middle-aged, but he juggled the finances of the company with extreme adroitness and the other two partners were well aware of the fact.

'Vyvyan Weighman's contract,' Fitzwarren led off. 'We've got to make up our minds what we are going to do about it.'

'I imagine he'll be looking for a substantial increase.'

'What I'm wondering is whether we should renew it at all.'

'Weighman's got talent, Toni.'

'When he wants to use it. And with all his talent he didn't land that pet food account for us, did he?'

'He fell out with their managing director.'

'Good grief, when you're going after an account you can't afford to fall out with managing directors. Let them have their whims, peculiarities, provincial accents, whatever. That's just Weighman's weakness, he gets bloody-minded. There was that business outside the Confrontation, remember? Black eyes and bloody noses and God knows what. Before he teamed up with us, thank goodness; it's not the sort of publicity any firm wants.'

'He probably gets his bloody-mindedness from his father.'

'Is the old boy still alive?'

'Must be; or Vyvyan wouldn't be doing a job. I know you don't really like him, Toni —'

'He doesn't really like me, so its mutual. The difference is that I'm polite enough to hide it most of the time; he isn't.'

'Well, like I said, I think he's talented. I think if he puts his mind to it he can do pretty well anything.'

'And I think he doesn't always put his mind to it, he doesn't care all that much. So what do we do?'

'You're the boss, Toni; it's up to you.'

When Vyvyan reached his own small office at the far end of the corridor, Kitty, the attractive young secretary whom he shared with another copy-writer, said, 'Mr Fitzwarren says would you look in and see him, Mr Weighman.'

Vyvyan nodded, but after twenty minutes he was still seated at his desk revising some draft copy.

The intercom buzzed.

'Weighman here,' he said.

'Did Kitty let you know I wanted a word with you?'

'She did say something about it. I'll be along.'

'Entirely at your own convenience, of course,' Tom said with heavy sarcasm.

Vyvyan seated himself comfortably in the green leather-covered chair and took stock of the man opposite him across the desk; in a flash of inspiration he realised that one reason why they didn't get on together could well be that they were too much alike in temperament . . .

'I was hoping for a talk with you,' he said.

'I did suggest it,' Toni pointed out, 'about half an hour ago.'

'I was busy on the copy for the Instant Tailoring ads.'

'Let's hope it works out more successful than the stuff you suggested for the breakfast food people.'

'You didn't like that?' Vyvyan asked quietly.

'It wasn't good.'

'There can always be two opinions about that, of course. Maybe it was too good.'

'As far as our job is concerned too good is as bad as not good enough. We've got to get the thing just *right*. Hit the *exactly* right note; *exactly* the right idiom; *exactly* the right phrase.'

'Well, suppose we leave the lecture on copy-writing for another time and talk about my contract.'

Fitzwarren carefully selected a cigarette from a silver box on his desk; lit it from an expensive-looking lighter; returned the lighter to the pocket of an elegant maroon-coloured waistcoat.

'I want the renewal to run for at least three years and I want more money.'

– Thinking back to the interview perched on a high bar stool in The Brave Bombardier an hour later Vyvyan could see that it was from that point (*'I want the renewal to run for at least three years and I want more money'*) that the

17

discussion began to deteriorate.

At different points both men lost their tempers and said things which would have been better left unsaid; then each tried to make some sort of amends after his own particular fashion and made an effort to patch up the rather badly cracked veneer of politeness.

Each was under a certain amount of background pressure. Toni Fitzwarren knew that his two partners both had a good opinion of Vyvyan's ability as a copy-writer; Vyvyan himself didn't want to have to go back to Hambledon Street that evening and tell Barbara that he was out of a job.

In the end an arrangement was arrived at, and in The Brave Bombardier Vyvyan realised that he was on the losing end of things.

What had been arranged was that Vyvyan was to continue on a temporary contract for three months at a slightly increased salary. At the end of three months the partners would have decided whether to offer him a long-term contract or not.

He could go back, therefore, to Chelsea and tell Barbara, 'I've got a little more money,' but if he were honest he would have to add, 'And in three months time I shall be out on my ear.'

Because, as he realised, that was what was going to happen. That bastard Fitzwarren didn't like him and would certainly talk the other two into getting rid of him ...

He regretted now that he hadn't told Fitzwarren to stuff his three months; it was rather out of character not to have done so.

Back in his own room he simply told Kitty, 'If anyone wants me, I'm out. I'll be back some time.'

He left the office, walked a short way along Bond Street and dodging down an alleyway known only to habituees arrived at The Brave Bombardier.

Vyvyan was good in pubs. The pub atmosphere suited him; even more deeply, the pub philosophy suited him. A man didn't feel rooted in a pub, and Vyvyan was typically modern in not liking roots. A man could come and go as he pleased, when he pleased; in and out; no questions asked, no explanations expected; this he liked; he liked, too, the comforting anonymity of a pub. The man next to you might stand staring at his drink and not say a word for half an hour; or he might, without encouragement or provocation, pour out to you whole chunks of most intimate life-history; it didn't matter, because he didn't know who you were, you didn't know him, and in all probability you would never see one another again. A man could sit up on his high stool, keep himself to himself, and see and hear some very odd types.

And, of course, at the Bombardier there was Mrs Bennett.

Presumably she had once been christened and had been given a first name, but nobody knew what it was, and it was very doubtful even if her christian name were known whether anyone would have been bold enough to use it.

Mrs Bennett was tall and straight-backed; she dyed her hair (you could occasionally see hints of a tell-tale darkness at the roots); she spoke in an accent which Vyvyan himself had once described as 'bogus Cheltenham grafted on to basic Commercial Road'; she had never been heard to make any remark which could, by any stretch of the imagination, be said to belong to the permissive age.

Yet, unlikely though it might be, this woman exuded femininity.

In her presence, even if he were too scared to say so, every man was aware of the fact that she was a woman and he was a man.

On Vyvyan she exercised a sort of fascination; more than once he had indulged in the extreme fantasy that if ever he got tired of Barbara (or she of him) he might fly for comfort to the arms and the forbidding bosom of Mrs Bennett.

What Mrs Bennett thought about her various customers

was unknown, the woman was as discreet in what she didn't say as any club hall porter of the old regime. She knew Vyvyan well by sight, and if she could have been induced to pass an opinion on him it would have been: 'A deep one, that Mr Weighman; up-to-date but deep, sort of dark, if you know what I mean.'

The only other occupant of the Saloon at that moment, Mrs Bennett did not know; nor did Vyvyan. A little man, finnicky in a poverty-stricken sort of way; an unexpected growth of beard covering his small chin; keen bright eyes darting their sharp glances everywhere, 'like a rat peering out of a lavatory brush,' Vyvyan thought.

'Aristotle was the pupil of Plato,' this odd little man remarked suddenly in a voice which was as unexpected as the words themselves, for he used the high-pitched, clear, thin, academic tones proper to an Oxford common room of a generation ago.

'I once said that in the public bar of an inn in a remote Yorkshire hamlet and after a moment of shocked silence the landlord called out reprovingly "Language, *please*," and the woman he was talking to said, "I'm a respectable married woman, I didn't come here to be insulted." '

'Mad as a coot,' Vyvyan thought; but he laughed because there was something incongruous and diverting about the little man's whole *persona*: his appearance, voice and what he said.

'Of course,' the rat behind the lavatory brush continued, 'the fellow turned out to be Pisces. An unreliable lot the Pisces. Untrustworthy. Dicey – is that the correct word these days? – dicey. It's all there; but people won't use it. Like having a book on the shelf and never opening it. It's all written down.' He glanced at Mrs Bennett, but was obviously and quite rightly intimidated, so he turned to Vyvyan instead.

'Now, I would guess you to be a Leo, sir.'

Vyvyan's birthday was August the ninth so, although still

firmly of the opinion that this character was pleasantly un-hinged, he couldn't help feeling mildly interested.

'And supposing I am,' he answered, 'what of it?'

'Ah, I can tell you what of it, sir, being a Leo myself. This will turn out to be a critical year for us Leos. Money matters; changes; big decisions.'

Vyvyan's big decision at the moment was to have the other half of his gin and tonic.

He pushed his glass across the counter and invited the self-appointed soothsayer to join him.

The little man accepted with alacrity.

'A glass of Madeira wine for me, sir. The dry Sercial. Have you any connection with Madeira, sir? Have you ever been there?'

Unexpectedly Mrs Bennett joined the conversation at this point.

'And where do you go for your holiday, if I may ask?' she inquired.

'Clacton.'

There was an incongruity between the word and the precise academic tones in which it was spoken that made Vyvyan and Mrs Bennett instinctively catch one another's eye and smile.

'And these big money matters,' Vyvyan asked. 'What does that mean? Am I going to win the Pools?'

'Ah, everybody wants to know that, sir. Pools-mad, that's what we have all become. The heavenly bodies are not concerned with the Pools. As a Leo I say that money matters loom large for us, sir, they loom large.'

'I hope they'll loom a bit larger than they are at present,' Vyvyan said, and Mrs Bennett caught his eye again and smiled sympathetically.

When eventually he got back to the office Kitty was as reproachful as she dared to be.

'There've been an awful lot of calls for you, Mr Weigh-man,' she told him. 'I've made a list and said you'd ring

21

back when you could. I said you were out at a conference.'

'Good girl, you'll go far.'

'Miss Courlander rang.'

'Miss Courlander?' Vyvyan was surprised; it was one of Barbara's quirks that she wanted to have no connection with Vyvyan's life at the office and never telephoned him there.

'Just after you'd gone out. But she said it was no good your ringing back because she had to go out for a long session at the hairdresser.'

'My God, woman and hair!'

'If you ask me it's men and hair these days,' Kitty replied spiritedly. 'My boy-friends spend as much on having their hair seen to as I do.'

'But they don't look so nice,' Vyvyan assured her. 'Now let's get on with these calls —'

He picked out what sounded like the most important of the calls and worked his way unenthusiastically through them. When he had finished he looked quickly through the folder containing his ideas for the Instant Tailoring copy and decided not to take it home with him. He had had enough of T.M. & F. for one day.

The evening was wet and cold. The thin, steady rain splashed up off the pavements and was spurted up from the gutters by the wheels of speeding buses and cars.

King's Road was noisy and unattractive, and Vyvyan was glad to turn out of it into the comparative quiet of Hambledon Street.

He let himself into the flat.

It was warm and bright and good to come back to.

In the intimate little living-room Barbara in her long red house-coat was sitting on the Regency stool in front of the gas-fire reading the *Evening Standard*. It was obvious at once that her session at the hairdresser's had been successful, and Vyvyan said so. He was not a man who normally paid compliments to his woman; he was inclined to take them for granted; but this evening he wanted Barbara to be in a good mood; he didn't relish telling her the outcome (or more correctly the lack of outcome) of his interview with Toni Fitzwarren.

'I hear you rang me?' he said.

Barbara put the *Standard* to one side (she had a passion for newsprint) and looked up.

'Yes, I did. I don't want to sound ghoulish about it but I'm not going to be hypocritical either. You can get out the champers. Your father's dead.'

'Good Lord, I thought the old boy would grind on for years yet. How did you hear?'

'They rang up from Chailey. And I told them I'd get in touch with you. It was heart apparently. He was walking back to the house across the lawn and suddenly collapsed and that was it.'

'I hope nobody expects me to shed any tears.'

'*I* don't. As I said, get out the champers. What about those two daughters of his by his second wife. Don't they live abroad? Madeira, or somewhere?'

'Yes, Madeira. Good Lord, that's odd —'

'What is?'

'Oh, nothing really. It was only that a character in the pub at midday was drinking Madeira and you don't often hear it asked for. What Zodiac sign are you, Bar?'

'Pisces. What's that got to do with anything?'

'Nothing. This chap in the pub was a sort of amateur astrologist. Obviously nuts. Only I will say for him he was right about big changes in money matters. This couldn't have happened at a better time for me. Changes indeed. I'll get a bottle. And after that a celebration dinner at the Lobster Pot, don't you think?'

Barbara nodded approvingly. 'And after the Lobster Pot,' she added, 'back home to bed. And not too late, either.'

III

Shortly after she had started to live with Vyvyan, Barbara Courlander had got herself a job in an antique shop close to Sloane Square. People were inclined to refer to the shop as Tooveys, but in fact it was somewhat whimsically christened The Two Vs, commemorating the names of the two partners – Christopher Vines and Peter Venning – who had set up in business there.

After a short while Vines had hived off on his own, leaving the Sloane Square shop in the sole care and possession of Peter Venning.

Venning was a man of forty with a corpulent flabby body and a flabby white face.

Barbara had no liking for the man, in fact there were even times when she felt slightly frightened by his soft sarcastic speech. As far as she knew no woman entered his life and if she thought about his sex life at all, and it wasn't a subject of any interest to her, she surmised that he was probably a neutral.

But Venning paid well; the shop was reasonably close to Hambledon Street; and the job was interesting, if only as an insight into how people could be conned into spending a great deal more money than they could really afford for something which had been brought through the back door of the shop for fifteen pounds and after a little 'adjustment' and titivating stood proudly in the front window marked seventy-five.

Venning was prepared to look at almost anything that the misused word 'antiques' could be stretched to cover; but, as with many such establishments, he had tended to make something of a speciality of one particular line.

Toovey's speciality was 'theatrical interest', anything which might be called 'nostalgia of the theatre', old play-bills, photographs, posters and so on, a section which gradually became extended to include some theatrical 'pro-perties' as well.

A week after the celebratory dinner in the Lobster Pot Barbara found herself less inclined than ever to put up with her employer's soft-spoken but envenomed sarcasms.

Vyvyan was that very morning due to meet the lawyer and executor to hear the terms of his father's will, and it was clear to Barbara that if she didn't want to continue with the job at the Two Vs there would be no need to do so.

Venning's sarcasm on this particular day was provoked by the repetition of a long-standing source of trouble – Barbara's inability to be quite sure of 'the code'.

In the tiny overcrowded room at the back of the shop which he used as an office Venning kept a book in which he religiously entered the actual price he paid for every article he purchased. The 'basic book' he called it. This purchase price was multiplied by whatever factor he judged cus-tomers could be persuaded to pay and the article in ques-tion was put into the shop with the resultant figure boldly displayed on a distinctive yellow label.

But since a number of customers liked to haggle there had to be room for manoeuvre, so on each yellow label, on the back or beneath the official price, appeared in much smaller writing an entry in code. This showed the lowest figure which might be accepted and below which no sale would be contemplated.

Thus a small china figure, bought perhaps in the sale of some minor establishment in the Home Counties, would be entered in the basic book at what had actually been paid for it, say £14.

Transferred into the window it would bear a yellow label plainly marked £38; underneath these figures, or possibly

25

on the reverse of the label, would appear the cryptic mark £ED.

In order to translate the code it was only necessary to remember the word GREYHOUNDS; starting with G for zero and R for one and so on each letter stood for a corresponding numeral. So the rule of the shop in this instance would run: ask £38 for the china figure and don't even look like abating the price unless you have to; but if an obvious hard bargainer comes in and we are having a bad day you can go down even as low as £28 – but not a penny lower.

Nobody could possibly accuse Barbara Courlander of being woolly-witted or ineffectual. She was neither; but she did occasionally find it difficult to remember the GREYHOUNDS business and was inclined to get the letters and figures wrong.

Having rescued her in the nick of time from making a mistake Peter Venning waited till the customer had left the shop and then said in his soft, slightly lisping way, 'It must be marvellous, Barbara dear, to be as well off as you and not to have to worry about the odd ten pounds.'

'I never am quite sure about that damned code.'

'Unfortunately I have to be. We haven't all got expectations from rich old gentlemen dying.'

'You heard about Vyvyan's father, then?'

'With envy. What a very comforting star you have hitched yourself to, haven't you, dear?'

Barbara smiled. In the circumstances she thought she could afford to put up with a few snide remarks from the unlovable Peter.

The letter from Manning & Dale, Solicitors, informed Vyvyan that his late father had appointed Barrolds bank to act as executors to the estate and that it would therefore be convenient, if Mr Weighman agreed, if the meeting to learn the provisions of the Will were held at Barrolds' West End branch where their executor department was situated.

Setting out for the job at the Two Vs that morning Barbara had bidden Vyvyan a cheerful farewell.

'Good luck, darling. Come back loaded.'

'Good grief, woman, you don't really expect them to hand the cash over straight away, in bags or something, do you?'

'A nice fat cheque will do.'

In an office on the first floor of Barrolds' West End branch two men sat waiting.

Archer, the head of the executive department of the bank, and Manning the family solicitor.

'You've acted for Sir Lucien for some time, I take it?' Archer asked. He had a round face and the rather particular eyes of a man whose heart would one day betray him suddenly.

'Yes, for fifteen years.' Manning was as neat and precise in his speech as in his person.

'Not the easiest of clients I should imagine?'

The lawyer smiled a '*de mortuis –*' smile. 'Let us say that all human beings have their whims.'

'And the son —'

'Mr Vyvyan Weighman.'

'Isn't he the man who got mixed up in some business outside a West End night club? I seem to remember reading something about it at the time.'

'The press made the most of it; although I'm not defending Weighman, he made a fool of himself.'

'I suppose he's one of the modern violent generation, is he?'

'He's certainly younger than we are.'

'I can't make out what the present lot are getting at. What they *want*. Chaos? No good asking me to understand them, I'm afraid. I don't. There are two daughters as well, aren't there?'

'By the second marriage. Mrs Selincourt, a widow, and

Miss Lucy Weighman, a spinster.'

'Are they coming today?'

'No. They both live in Funchal, Madeira, and have done for some years now.'

'They are beneficiaries as well, I presume?'

Manning, who didn't like the bank official much, had no intention of disclosing the contents of the Will until the proper time.

'All three are certainly beneficiaries under the Will,' was all he was prepared to say.

Vyvyan arrived on time, not by any means a guaranteed performance by him because exact punctuality was not his strong suit.

He had met Manning before, although only once; and he took an instant dislike to the Barrolds' bank official.

The conventional phrases of introduction and polite inquiry were ritualistically observed.

'How do you do?' Vyvyan asked of Mr Archer, thinking, even as he uttered the meaningless words, that he couldn't care less how the pop-eyed, pot-bellied, balding, boring little nonentity did.

'A sad occasion, I'm afraid,' Mr Archer felt constrained to say.

'Not for me,' Vyvyan assured him.

Mr Archer didn't trouble to hide his distaste for the remark.

'Well now,' the lawyer put in tactfully, 'shall I begin? You probably understand, Mr Weighman, that your two half-sisters, Mrs Selincourt and Miss Lucy Weighman, will not be here today because of their residence abroad, in Madeira ('... *a glass of Madeira wine for me, sir. The dry Sercial ... money matters loom large, sir; they loom large ...*') but I shall of course be writing to them severally either today or tomorrow to acquaint them with the details of your father's Will.'

'I'm not interested in my half-sisters,' Vyvyan assured

him. 'Never have been.'

Mr Archer was shocked. 'At the same time they must be informed as to the contents of the Will,' he said.

'Manning has already said he will do that,' Vyvyan pointed out, 'so that's fixed. Can we get on with the business?'

Manning cleared his throat.

'Your late father has left a considerable estate,' he said. 'It isn't possible to put an exact figure on death duties at the moment, but they can be estimated with reasonable accuracy, and even putting them at the highest probable figure it seems certain that after they have been satisfied the net amount to be divided among a few bequests and the three beneficiaries – that is yourself, Mr Weighman, and your two half-sisters – it seems certain that this amount will not be less than two hundred and eighty thousand pounds.'

Vyvyan tried to keep his face impassive. But it was difficult. A total of two hundred and eighty thousand was more than he had dared hope for. He was under the impression that his old fool of a father had blued most of his money away . . . Of course there were the half-sisters in Funchal to think about, but even if you had to divide two hundred and eighty thousand by three . . . *come back loaded*, Barbara had said . . .

After his preliminary remarks Manning was now producing the Will itself.

'This is the last Will and Tesmament —'

Intoning it . . . just like a scene from a film, Vyvyan thought; mumbo-jumbo. But if this particular piece of mumbo-jumbo was going to put some seventy thousand pounds into his lap he was all in favour of it. Long live Mumbo-Jumbo . . .

The few incidental bequests which the lawyer had spoken of he now read out in detail.

Vyvyan totalled them roughly in his head as they were particularised. Less than three thousand pounds. Not a matter of any real significance when the splendid total of two hundred and eighty thousand was glowing on the horizon.

'... in trust —' the lawyer was continuing '... power to call in, sell or convert as may seem fit and proper ... my estate both real and personal ... the resultant sum to be divided as follows, that is to say: to my son Vyvyan Prendergast Weighman the sum of two hundred and fifty pounds; and to my daughters Henrietta (now known as Henrietta Selincourt) and Lucy, both at present resident in Madeira, the whole of the remainder in equal proportion between them...'

The lawyer finished by reading the names of the two witnesses and the date of the signing and then there was silence in the room.

The hum of the West End traffic came steadily even through the double glazing of the windows.

Archer was studying Vyvyan's face ... *that's set him back a bit* he thought ...

Vyvyan was indeed set back. He felt quite stunned. In fact for the first few seconds his mind couldn't accept what his ears had received.

When he spoke he only just had control of his voice.

'Are you telling me,' he asked, 'that all I am going to get from my father's estate is two hundred and fifty pounds? That can't be the case, surely?'

'I'm afraid it is, Mr Weighman.'

'But – *two hundred and fifty pounds!* It's nothing. *Nothing!*'

The lawyer spread his hands almost apologetically; Barrolds' bank man even smiled slightly. Vyvyan looked at them both in cold fury and without saying another word got up and walked out of the room.

IV

Vyvyan had a long-standing engagement for the week-end following the disastrous reading of his father's Will.

Barbara's reaction to the news about the Will matched his own: plain disbelief at first quickly hardening into cold fury.

'The Barrolds' bank man wanted to say it served me right for not being a dutiful bum-sucking son, I could see that.'

'Sanctimonious sod,' Barbara said. 'If you had been left only *a third* – what's that? Seventy thousand-odd, isn't it? God Almighty, just imagine, seventy thousand!'

After a pause she went on, 'Well, you'll have to screw more than ever out of T.M. & F. now, won't you?'

'That won't work for long,' Vyvyan said and he went on to tell her the details of his unsatisfactory arrangement with Toni Fitzwarren, matters which he had conveniently been able to slur over up till now since the news of his father's death had driven other affairs into the background.

Barbara listened gloomily and at the end her only comment was, 'You're beginning to come unstuck as a money making machine, aren't you, darling?'

Vyvyan set off for his week-end in the country by no means certain that he would find Barbara waiting for him in Hambledon Street when he came back. That was a problem which could only be solved when the week-end was over, meanwhile it lay ahead of him, to be spent in a comfortable house with agreeable people and he intended to enjoy it.

The Court House, Amminster Green, lay in the middle of farming land some five miles away from the old-fashioned little country town of Amminster.

Vyvyan's hosts were Alan Plowman and his wife Nancy.

Plowman was one of those thin, loosely built Englishmen who somehow continue to make you think of horses even when they aren't mounted on one, and who, since the forests of Burma and the Civil Service of India are no longer open to them, have taken to farming, usually very successfully, in the English countryside.

Nancy was a splendid partner: practical, energetic, hardworking, commonsensical; the genus *memsahib* at its best.

Together they made excellent hosts.

Conventionally polite things were said about Vyvyan's father, and when Vyvyan abruptly turned the conversation neither of them thought it was from any excess of grief.

Bridge was the feature of the week-end to which Vyvyan was looking forward with the greatest pleasure. The gambling card games – chemin de fer, baccarat and the like – had little interest for him. He considered that too much depended on mere chance and he was a man who liked to organise and plan his own destiny.

At the bridge table he was a first-rate partner and a formidable opponent, and it was considerably on account of his prowess at the game that Nancy Plowman had invited him for the week-end.

Among her many *memsahib* virtues bridge playing came high.

If she was not quite as good a player as Vyvyan she was at least good enough to play with him and mightily enjoyed doing so. Alan was wise enough not to play.

Briefing Vyvyan about the evening's arrangements before the two other guests arrived for dinner Nancy had to confess to a minor disappointment.

'Muriel Benson was coming – she's the wife of the bank manager in Amminster and a really frightfully good player, almost as good as you are, Vyvyan, but she had to cry off. Her au pair has left her; walked out, just like that; and she simply can't get another. They all want to go to London and simply won't look at places like Amminster; though actually the Bensons don't live in the town, about two miles out; quite a nice little house with a field; they've got a pony and the two children ride, that is to say when they've got someone to go out with them; Muriel couldn't ride a donkey on Blackpool sands, bless her. But she can play bridge.'

'Does that mean we shan't have a four?' Vyvyan inquired in alarm.

'Good heavens, no. I've got a four all right. I wouldn't let you down to that extent. You; me; Rupert Storey, who's the local industrial magnate round here, so that's at least three reasonable players, and when Muriel dropped out I got a man from Amminster University, a Professor Leonard Davidson.'

'I didn't know there was a University of Amminster.'

'Oh Lord yes. Complete with all the modern trimmings – sit-ins and demos and student power and so on. We've got to know one or two of the faculty there; and this Leonard Davidson creature, who is obviously highly intelligent, claims to play bridge. He may be international class for all I know.'

Dinner was a highly enjoyable meal; whatever Nancy Plowman turned her hand to she tried to do really well, and usually she succeeded. Cooking was no exception and with a perfectly cooked *coq-au-vin* as the main dish and a bottle of really excellent Burgundy circulating Vyvyan thought, characteristically, not of how lucky he was, but once again of how monstrously unfair it was that he had been robbed, no less, of an inheritance which would have guaranteed the pleasant life for him for the rest of his days.

Dinner over, Alan retired to his study and the other four gratefully got down to the serious business of the evening.

Vyvyan already knew Nancy's play: on the good side of average; very steady; very dependable; no 'psyches' or fancy tricks. With her as your partner you weren't likely to bring off any sensational coups, on the other hand you would never find yourself landed in some complete disaster. Storey, the local industrial king, turned out to be the same sort of steady dependable player with perhaps just a slight tendency to be dazzled by the sight of a lot of high cards in his hand.

Leonard Davidson, Reader in Social History at the University of Amminster, was a less standardised individual altogether and it showed in his bridge. His calling was gloriously unpredictable; he made some calls which left Vyvyan gasping by their utter indefensibility, but he was quite likely in the next hand to redeem himself and earn his partner's grateful thanks by landing a high contract by play which – if it wasn't a sheer fluke and Vyvyan never felt sure on the point – could only be described as absolutely brilliant.

Altogether it was a highly enjoyable session and when the last rubber was finished and the scores totted up Alan Plowman came in from his self-imposed exile in the study to sit and chat over final drinks.

The bridge table, which is so often a battlefield of accusations and recriminations, had been a friendly affair, its various interchanges conducted in an atmosphere far less acrimonious than that which now suddenly developed in the conversation.

It became clear that Rupert Storey didn't think anything at all of modern universities in general and certainly nothing of the University of Amminster in particular.

It became equally clear that Leonard Davidson didn't think much of modern industrialists, or of the general framework of the society into which they were so integrally fitted.

Their host seemed genuinely interested in the somewhat heated discussion which sprang up; Nancy Plowman hovered on the edge of it, her only real anxiety being that things shouldn't blow up into a socially embarrassing scene. Vyvyan listened with only mild interest; like many men of his generation and background he felt absolutely no call to side with, or defend, the existing framework of society on the grounds of loyalty or tradition; but neither could he work up any enthusiasm for some radical change which could hardly be expected to bring him any benefit personally.

'... the whole unfolding of history,' Davidson maintained (now in full professional spate), 'has been a struggle for power. And that has very largely meant a struggle for property. At the Reformation the Crown seized property from the Church. A good or bad thing according to how you look at it. The Enclosure Acts took property away from the peasants. A bad thing by any reckoning. The Industrial Revolution took the ownership of the means of production into a comparatively few hands. From which we are now suffering. Distributivist. It's a hideous word and maybe that's why we are unpopular. But that's what I am, a distributivist.'

Rupert Storey could hardly wait to chip in. 'But, Good Lord, this is all theoretical nonsense. Typical modern university stuff. *I'm* the distributivist, if you want to use the wretched word.'

'You?'

'Certainly I am. What property do you distribute, anyway? But I *do*. This Friday morning for instance, and every single Friday morning throughout the year, I go to Barrolds' bank in the High Parade, Amminster; or more accurately somebody goes there for me, and we draw out the best part of thirty thousand pounds. By five o'clock on the same afternoon that has gone out, *been distributed,* in some twelve hundred pay packets. By seven o'clock next day, Saturday, it's safe to say that over eighty per cent of that money has found its way into the shops of the district, spent by over twelve hundred housewives.

'That goes on every week because I've got the know-how to build up a business and the ability to keep it running.

35

'Thirty thousand pounds a week; where would the neighbourhood be without it? If that isn't the distribution of property I'd like to know what is.'

'What I am afraid you fail to appreciate —'

Nancy Plowman caught Vyvyan's eye and her slight suggestion of a smile said *Oh Lord, these hobby-horsers! I wish we had played one more rubber now* . . .

Vyvyan smiled back politely, but neither of them had to endure much more argument for Storey caught sight of the clock and bethought himself of an early start he had to make in the morning.

The heat of discussion was turned off and polite farewells and thanks were spoken.

Vyvyan and his hosts sat for a few minutes over a final night-cap watching the still friendly embers of a dying wood fire.

When by general consent they all made a move upstairs Nancy Plowman said, 'Good night, Vyvyan. I do hope you have all you want in your room. Sleep well. Do you think over various hands you played before going off?'

Vyvyan admitted that he often did. 'The great value of bridge,' he said, 'is that it stops you thinking about other things.'

But in point of fact on that particular evening, as he lay in an unfamiliar bed staring up into the darkness above him, it was not bridge but 'other things' which mainly occupied his thoughts.

Next morning, Saturday, Alan Plowman announced, 'I've got to take the Land-Rover into Amminster to get some stakes and some binder twine. What about coming along, Vyvyan? We can do my bit of shopping and then look in at the Lion for the odd half-pint.'

'An absolutely excellent idea,' Nancy said. 'You two men go off on your pub crawl and leave a hard-working woman free to see to things in the house.'

'One of the secrets of being a husband,' Alan remarked as they made their way to the barn converted into a garage at the back of the house, 'is to know when you are not wanted.'

On the way to Amminster the Land-Rover had a third occupant: Bruce, a large, jet-black Labrador with all the dignity and good manners of his breed.

The hamlet of Amminster Green was separated from the town itself by a good five miles and the country between the two was almost entirely agricultural. As Amminster grew nearer houses became a little more frequent.

'That's where Benson lives,' Alan said pointing one out. 'The Bank Manager. His wife was to have been one of your bridge four last night, remember?'

Vyvyan looked out of the car window with interest and saw an inoffensive but unambitious house built in the modern idiom standing by itself next to a small wood.

He could see a garage to the right of the house and beyond the garage a field with a pony grazing in it.

'What sort of chap is Benson?' he asked.

Alan seemed slightly surprised by the question. 'What sort? I hardly know him really, and Nancy only comes across his wife because of bridge. I'd say he's a mild, harmless sort of little chap.'

'Do you bank there?'

'No. I use Barclays at the far end of the town. Are you a Barrolds man?'

'No. I can't say I like Barrolds.'

'Rupert Storey seems satisfied with them.'

'Where is his factory?'

'The other side of Amminster. One of the light industries. Small electrical stuff. He's probably their biggest customer I would think. Well, what did he say, twelve hundred pay packets and over thirty thousand quid a week to pay out?'

'That's quite a useful sum of money,' Vyvyan said

thoughtfully.

Amminster was proud of the fact that it didn't possess a High Street but boasted a High Parade instead. Halfway along it Alan brought the Land-Rover to a halt and said, 'Here's Mostyn's where I get my stuff. I hope not to be more than a minute or two. You might sit tight if you don't mind and if a traffic warden comes along do your best to fend him off. Say I'm getting urgent agricultural supplies and I'll be out in a minute.'

Vyvyan nodded. 'Will do,' he agreed.

Bruce sat up for a moment in some concern at the departure of his god and obviously only accepted the lesser mortal's reassurances as an unsatisfactory second-best.

Having spoken a soothing word to the dog Vyvyan turned his attention to the street scene about him.

Except in name Amminster's High Parade was pretty well a replica of any other small country town High Street now standardised up and down England.

Farther along on the left-hand side Vyvyan could see the noble sign of The White Lion hanging proudly over the pavement. The red and gold front of a Woolworth's was rather glaringly visible; not far from it was a Timothy Whites. A dry-cleaning establishment stood next to a Home Co. furnishing store and beyond that was the inevitable television and radio shop. Almost exactly opposite Mostyn's Ironmongery & General Agricultural store where, at that very moment, Alan was doing his best to hurry up the purchase of stakes and binder twine, stood Barrolds bank.

Vyvyan studied it with interest.

A small building, clearly one of Barrolds least important branches; two windows fronting the street, a door with an entrance porch; an entry at the side which seemed to lead to some sort of yard.

Not by any means an imposing or intimidating sort of place Vyvyan thought . . .

'Any wardens?' Alan asked anxiously reappeared encumbered with his purchases.

Vyvyan reassured him and got out to help with storing the binder twine and stakes in the back.

Bruce agreed, with evidently wounded dignity, to make way for the intruding goods.

'We'll have a quick pint at the Lion and pick up an *Advertiser* on the way home,' Alan said.

At the Court House after lunch Nancy took up the *Advertiser*, as she did every week, and read it thoroughly. A number of local happenings – W.I. meetings, Red Cross fêtes and the like – had interest for her.

Looking through the advertisement columns she was moved to say, 'Poor Mrs Benson; no end of people are advertising for au pairs and helps and so on, but there's never a single one asking for a job.'

When Vyvyan got back to Hambledon Street he found Barbara toasting her long shapely legs in front of the gas-fire.

She looked up as he entered.

'The rat's still here,' she greeted him. 'How's the ship?'

He laughed; when she wanted to be she was an exciting piece of femininity for a man to come back to.

'Not quite sinking yet,' he said.

'Did you make vast sums of money at bridge?'

'I ended up just over a quid to the good.'

'Riotous times ahead, I can see that.'

Vyvyan laughed easily and Barbara looked at him a little curiously. 'You don't seem particularly worried about things,' she said.

'What's the good of worrying?'

Barbara joined him in laughing, then, 'You're absolutely right,' she agreed. 'To hell with it all.' She held out her glass. 'A large one please, darling, and then we'll go out to the Pot.'

'I was just going to suggest that.'

'Two minds that think as one.'

'And back not too late.'

'Two minds still thinking as one.'

'Tonight I want to come back early to talk. There's something I want to ask you about.'

Gustave, who ran the Lobster Pot, was as pleased as ever to see two of his regular customers, and two, moreover, whom he regarded as ideal Lobster Pottites – the right age, the right appearance, the right amount of money to spend.

On this particular evening they disappointed him a little by not lingering as usual over their Remy Martins.

The Lobster Pot boasted of its 'intimate atmosphere' which in plainer English meant that it was minute and usually hideously overcrowded so that not only was your neighbour's elbow likely to be in your ribs but it was only too easy for his ear, however unintentionally, to tune in to what you were saying.

Vyvyan therefore refused to say anything during the meal in enlargement of his somewhat mysterious remark about having 'something I want to ask you about', and it was Barbara, filled with ever-increasing curiosity, who decided, much to Gustave's regret, to cut out the Remy Martins for once and get back to Hambledon Street.

'You are in a 'urry to go, perhaps?' Gustave said.

Barbara smiled brightly at him. 'This evening we are in a bit of a hurry to get back, yes.'

Gustave made a Gallic gesture – that slight movement of the hands and shoulders which recognises the inevitability of life; accepts it; glories in it.

'I understand this vair well,' he said.

On the way out Barbara, amused, said, 'Does that man ever think of anything else?'

'Food, sometimes, obviously. Look, when we get back fix some coffee, will you? And I'll say my little piece.'

When coffee was made and the gas-fire turned up to its full, Vyvyan said, 'You remember that novel-launching

40

party I went to when you didn't come along?'

Barbara nodded.

'And after it I gave Philip Manderville, the actor, a lift home and sat talking for a bit with him and his barrister chum. I'm not sure now how we got on to the subject but we talked for quite a bit about the perfect crime —'

Barbara gave a gasp of astonished amusement, 'Don't tell me you've committed one?' she cried.

'No. Not yet.'

'Not yet?'

'The barrister fellow said that in the end the criminal gets caught; but I said he needn't; and I still think he needn't. I think the reason things go wrong is because there's very seldom enough preparation. I'm a great believer in the Trojan Horse method.'

'Expound a bit. My French history never was very strong.'

'If you are going to get away with it you have somehow got to worm your way right into the enemy's camp and have a jolly good look round before you decide to do anything at all. And this is where I want you to help me, if you're willing to.'

'Don't be silly, darling. Of course I'm willing. I couldn't be more excited. I'm game for anything. I just want to hear what it is, that's all.'

'But look, Bar, there may not be a dangerous part of course; the whole thing may be a non-starter; but if we do get it off the ground and there *is* any danger, you aren't to be mixed up in that part of it.'

'Oh my God, you sound like your Victorian grandfather. What's the good of anything unless there's some sort of risk, danger, attached to it? No danger, no fun. Who the hell wants to go ski-ing in Battersea Park? What is it you want me to do?'

'Take a temporary job.'

'What sort of a job?'

'Half companion, half au pair, and there'll be two kids to teach riding to. You'll like that part of it.'

Barbara stared at him a little uncertainly, 'What an extraordinary man you are,' she said. 'Where is all this to be?'

'Here's how you set about it,' Vyvyan explained. 'As soon as may be, tomorrow if you can, you take the Volvo down to Amminster and find the offices of the local paper, the *Advertiser*. I'm not sure where they are, but it's a small place and you won't have any difficulty in finding them. I suppose there'll be a girl inside taking classified advertisements. You'll have one ready. We'll draft it out this evening. "*Young woman, country lover, good with horses, able to look after children. Cheerful and willing.*" That sort of thing —'

'Good God, have I got all those attributes?' Barbara asked.

'Only about some things,' Vyvyan assured her, grinning. 'You'll do this under an assumed name of course and without any address, just a box number.

We'll have to wait a week or ten days because the *Advertiser* only comes out weekly, then you'll go there again and pick up your answers.'

'Suppose there aren't any?'

'Don't worry. There'll be a dozen at least. And among them there'll be one from a Mrs Benson.'

'And who is Mrs Benson?'

Vyvyan, who had a good sense of dramatic timing, slowly chose and lit a cigarette before replying with deliberate casualness.

'She's the wife of the local bank manager.'

Barbara stared at him for a moment in speculation and then asked, 'Wouldn't this be the point in an old-style melodrama where I ought to say, "*You begin to interest me strangely*"?'

'Mr Benson, whom I have never seen yet, is the manager of the Amminster Branch of Barrolds Bank.'

'Barrolds?'

Vyvyan nodded and Barbara smiled slightly.

'How very appropriate,' she said.

'Things do work out to a pattern sometimes.'

'And what am I supposed to do exactly?'

Vyvyan dropped all the banter out of his tone and said, 'Listen, Bar: it's quite likely that nothing will come of this. I've only got half an idea in my head, anyway. No sort of real plan yet. Except' – a smile flickered across his face – 'a plan to assist in a redistribution of property to a certain extent.'

'What does that mean exactly?'

'Well, it could mean nearly thirty thousand quid.'

'*Thirty thousand pounds?*'

'It's a possibility if – and only if – we go about it the right way from the beginning. What you've got to do first is to get this companion-help-au-pair job in the Bensons' household.

'I'm convinced that that won't be difficult for you to do. Once you are installed I want you to watch everything, get *au fait* with everything. The times that everything happens. The sort of car Benson uses. What his schedule is each morning, when he goes off to the bank and so on. *And keys*. What he does about his keys. Where does he keep them? Put them at night? Has he got an alarm from his house to the police station? What sort of staff is there at the bank? Anything, everything.'

'Am I supposed to seduce the man?'

'If it's going to help. And, you never know your luck, it might not be necessary, he might try to rape you. Some of these bank managers are devils once you get them away from their overdrafts.'

'Country-lover,' Barbara said. 'Cheerful and willing. I couldn't be more excited. Well, I'll have a go at it anyway.'

V

James Benson turned his Morris 1100 into the gateway of 'Wenlock' at five past six. Give or take a few minutes this was his normal time for getting back from the bank every evening.

The bank closed its doors to the public in Amminister High Parade at three; but after the customers had been shut out there still remained a great deal, even in a small branch, to be done every day. Balances had to be struck, cash verified, the last of the letters signed and the manager had to see that everything was locked up safely before he finally felt free to go home.

All this routine of departure – just like its counterpart in the morning, the routine of opening up – was done methodically.

Little James Benson was a great man for method and order. If everything was always kept in its right place nothing got lost; if things were always done in the right sequence nothing got forgotten.

There had been moments in their married life when this love of precision on her husband's part – *'James's fussiness'* sometimes she called it – irked Muriel Benson; but such moments came far less frequently now than they used to do.

She had become inured to 'James's fussiness'; in fact she had become to some extent infected by it. They had been married for fifteen years and until three years ago Muriel Benson had been contentedly happy. Then James had been transferred to Amminster with promotion to the position of bank manager there.

There was never any thought of not accepting the bank's

offer of promotion-plus-transfer.

James had never been a man burning with ambition, and although Amminster was only a small branch he realised that at his age (he was forty-seven when he transferred there) it was the best plum he could expect to get out of the pie, and he made up his mind to be content with it.

After all, a manager was still a manager even if it was of a small, relatively unimportant branch.

In one respect the Bensons were lucky in coming to Amminister; they found a house and, aided by the bank, were able to buy it.

'Wenlock', as their house had been called by the exile from the Shropshire hills who had originally built it, was a pleasantly ordinary building standing some two miles out of the town along the Amminster Green road.

It had two rooms and a modernised kitchen on the ground floor; four bedrooms; and a garden where everything was snipped and trimmed and weeded with military exactness. The Bensons had been able to rent a two-acre field at the back of the house in which Polly the children's pony grazed.

But from another aspect, the move to Amminster proved troublesome, almost disastrous, for Muriel Benson.

Where they had lived previously she had been, as she now ruefully realised, extraordinarily lucky. Within five minutes walk of them there had been living a middle-aged widow who for a modest sum had been perfectly content to come in daily and tackle pretty well any job that had to be done, including the all-important one of keeping an eye on the children when Muriel Benson wanted to be out playing bridge.

At 'Wenlock', all by itself two miles out of the town, things were very different, and Muriel Benson's three years there had been one long history of domestic difficulties.

The most permanent arrangement she had been able to make was for a woman to come in three mornings a week, for two hours a time, who in a grudging, slap-dash way dealt with a certain amount of the housework. Help with the children had proved much more difficult to get, and Muriel was becoming sick and tired of paying for advertisements which often didn't attract a single reply, and then of trying to cope with the totally unsatisfactory girls who did occasionally turn up.

James Benson realised that his wife was having a trying time and did his best, after his fashion, to make allowances. But he didn't find it altogether easy; he was not an imaginative man and he hated routine to be upset ... 'Oh dear, James does like everything *just-so*,' Muriel would sometimes say plaintively to her friends.

Their married life had not been tempestuous; but then neither of them would have had it so, neither of them was built for tempests; and James would sometimes reflect rather complacently on his good fortune. Driving his Morris back from Amminster, the bank safely shut up and 'put to bed', behind him, he would think himself a happy man ... a managership (albeit a minor one); a neat little house; a happy marriage; two healthy children ... 'If only we could find somebody to give Muriel a hand occasionally', he would think, frowning a little as he contemplated the only cloud on his horizon ...

He turned his car into the gateway of 'Wenlock' at four minutes past six and brought it to rest in the garage noticing, as he did so, that there was a small patch of oil on the garage floor.

This worried him slightly and he made a mental note that he would have to get the place cleaned up.

Penny and Ursula were at the far end of the field with the pony; he waved to them and went indoors wondering, a little apprehensively, what luck Muriel had had in her latest effort to get somebody.

When Muriel had first seen the entry in the *Advertiser* she had cried out almost in disbelief.

'James, there's somebody actually wanting a job! Just exactly the sort of person we are looking for. Do listen: *"Young woman, country lover, good with horses and children, seeks position of companion au pair type in pleasant house. Cheerful willing worker. Friendly conditions more important than big salary. Reply Box 3X012."* '

'There you are then,' James replied. 'They do exist, after all. Are you going to answer it?'

'*Of course* I am. Now; this minute. You can drop it into the *Advertiser* offices on your way to the bank tomorrow morning. But she'll get dozens of replies; sure to. Somebody else is bound to snap her up, I'm afraid; bound to.'

'Not like you to be pessimistic, dear.'

His wife's reply had an unusual note of bitterness in it. 'After three years in this place of trying to get somebody to help me with the children I'm really beginning to feel pessimistic,' she said.

She had replied at length to the incredible advertisement and James had left 'Wenlock' a few minutes earlier next morning so that he could go round by the *Advertiser* offices and leave her letter there.

Muriel's pessimism was still on her. 'I'm afraid that's the last we shall hear about it,' she said, as she handed him the envelope. 'It's just too good to be true.'

It was in fact too good to be true; but Muriel Benson could hardly be expected to realise how accurate her assessment of the situation was, especially when, after four days of waning hope, she got a letter from a Miss Beryl Carpenter suggesting an interview.

It was this interview about which James was now expecting to hear.

'Well, did you meet her, dear?' he asked.

He knew the answer before his wife spoke; Muriel was looking happier and younger than for some time past.

'Yes, indeed I did. We had a cup of coffee together at Fenners and then I got a taxi from Wilson's garage and brought her out here to look at the house. And, James, *she's coming.*'

'She is? Oh, good. Splendid.'

'At least I'm almost certain that she is. She's going to ring up and confirm it; but she seemed so pleased with everything that I really do think she'll come.'

'And what's she like?'

'Oh dear,' Muriel gave a little laugh, 'I suppose one ought not to be surprised at anything these days, and of course all sorts of people do all sorts of jobs. But she's certainly not like the ordinary au pair one is used to. Not a bit. She's much more mature and – and well – *impressive* in every way. And very friendly. We couldn't have got on better together.'

James was delighted at his wife's obvious enthusiasm. 'What's her name again?' he asked.

'Beryl Carpenter.'

'What sort of age?'

'She told me that straight out, twenty-six.'

'And what's her history? Do we know anything about her?'

'Oh yes, she was absolutely frank about it all. Her father's a clergyman somewhere in Lincolnshire and she has been doing a secretarial job in London. She has got tired of living in town and wants to get into the country again where she can do some riding. Apparently she's very keen on horses. She was quite honest about not wanting to stay here for ever if she comes, but she said she would guarantee to stay for at least a year and very probably eighteen months.'

'Well, that's something.'

'Indeed it is.'

'And you think she will come?'

Muriel held up superstitiously crossed fingers.

'Yes, I do. And, James, do you know what I really think?'

Her husband was intrigued by the sudden lowering of her voice.

'What?'

'I think Beryl has had an unhappy love affair in London and wants to come into the country to get over it.'

'It sounds intriguing.'

'Mind you don't start making eyes at her,' Muriel warned rogueishly. 'She's good-looking enough.'

The fifty-year-old, non-passionate bank manager smiled slightly. 'That's hardly likely,' he said.

All the same, the fifty-year-old, non-passionate bank manager found that the presence of another woman in the house was definitely, and pleasantly, disturbing.

That Beryl Carpenter was feminine there could not be any possible doubt; the quasi-masculine clothes she habitually wore – corduroy slacks and an open-necked shirt – merely succeeded in emphasising the fact; with her in the house there was suddenly an infusion of essential femininity into the atmosphere of 'Wenlock' which James had never been conscious of before.

But what James Benson liked most was that the newcomer to the house was so friendly. He had never been good at making friends, and had always fought shy of the hearty, beer-swilling, pub-frequenting, over-masculine set that provided companionship for a lot of men.

Now he found that the extremely attractive girl of twenty-six who had miraculously, as it seemed, turned up out of the blue to help Muriel in her difficulties was perfectly willing to give him a hand in the garden whenever she was free to do so.

Not only willing, but enthusiastic.

Whatever the job was – clipping the front hedge, making up the bonfire, even creosoting the outside of the garage – she seemed anxious to take part.

It was agreeable, too, to have somebody who was really appreciative of what he did.

That Muriel was a dutiful and devoted wife fifteen years

of placid and on the whole happy marriage did not allow him to doubt; but when he had finished an hour's work in the garden she never came running out to say, 'Oh, James, what a *marvellous* job you have made of that.'

But Beryl did.

'Mr Benson, what a *marvellous* job you have made of that,' she cried looking with admiration at the mathematically level top of the box hedge. 'Super. It really is. You *are* clever.'

It was very agreeable to be called clever by an attractive girl of twenty-six.

'I'm sure you could do it just as well.'

'I certainly could *not*. I'd never keep it straight in a hundred years.'

Muriel liked being taken out in the car but she never took part in washing it; never even commented on how clean it looked when it had been washed.

Beryl borrowed overalls that hung up in the back of the garage and asked, 'Can I give a hand?'

And when it was finished and the Morris gleamed and shone in the evening sunshine, 'You do everything so *thoroughly* Mr Benson. I suppose it comes of being a bank manager.

'I suppose it does. Rather too prim and precise I'm afraid a lot of people would say.'

'Oh Lord, *I* don't. I admire it. I'm so much the other way, you know, haphazard, unpunctual. Now you, for instance, always leave for the bank at exactly the same time each morning, don't you?'

James smiled with a good deal of self-satisfaction. He prided himself on his methodical punctuality, and it was extremely pleasant to be admired for it.

'My dear Miss Carpenter,' he began a little pompously.

'Try Beryl, won't you?'

James looked startled.

'It's so much more friendly.'

'Oh well, if I may; yes, it *is* more friendly. You're quite right. Well, then, my dear Beryl, in my position as bank manager, I *have* to be punctual and methodical. This particular branch still opens at ten to the public and the staff come in at half past nine. I like to get there half an hour before that. Some of the younger men coming up in the bank nowadays tell me it's silly; but I suppose I have to say that I belong to the old-fashioned school. It means a lot to me to have that half hour to myself before the staff begin to come in. For one thing it sets a good example, if they know I'm there waiting the staff aren't likely to be late; and it gives me a chance to take a look round and open things up and generally clear the decks ready for action. So, as you know, I leave here at ten minutes to nine every morning. It's just a matter of training myself to be punctual.'

'I think it's marvellous how you do it. I suppose you have quite a big staff to look after, too?'

'Amminster is only a small branch, you know. And of course there is a general staff shortage everywhere. Young people aren't so keen on coming into banks these days it seems. Still, I do have three men and five girls under me, and that's quite enough to worry about at times.'

'I'm sure it is,' Beryl agreed admiringly.

After three weeks Beryl asked for, and was immediately granted, her first day off.

'Of course,' Muriel Benson agreed. 'Of course, any time you want.'

'I don't know if Mr Benson could give me a lift into Amminster in the morning? Then I could catch the ten-fifteen train.'

James said he would be delighted.

'I'll be ready at ten to nine exactly,' Beryl assured him, laughing.

At ten minutes to nine next morning James started the motor of his Morris 1100, with Beryl sitting in the passenger's seat beside him.

On the way into Amminster he said, 'I hope you are going to have a nice day, Beryl. I'm sure you deserve it. I can't tell you what a difference your being with us has made to Muriel. You are going to meet a friend perhaps in London?'

'My brother,' the girl beside him lied with instant and enthusiastic fluency. 'He lives in Lincolnshire near my parents and we don't see one another very often these days. I expect we shall go to a cinema, or perhaps even a matinee. Or maybe just sit and talk somewhere.'

When they reached the High Parade James turned the car neatly into the entrance by the side of the bank and brought it to a halt at the rear of the building now out of sight of the street.

'We're marvellously lucky having this little private yard,' he said. 'No parking difficulty, or trouble with wardens.'

'I suppose all the rest of the staff can use it too?'

'Only two of them are allowed to. I had to say "no" to the rest. It did create a bit of bad feeling at the time, but if I let everybody in the place would be chock-a-block.'

'You're a strict disciplinarian,' Beryl teased him.

'One has to have rules,' James defended himself with a return to his best pompous manner; as they got out of the car he said, 'I do hope you find your brother well and have a pleasant day in London with him.'

Barbara found her 'brother' in his pyjamas and a silk dressing-gown making coffee in the tiny kitchen in Hambledon Street.

'For God's sake give me a cup,' she said. 'I've hardly had a cup of coffee since I've been at the place. The Bensons are tea fiends. Tea at breakfast, and that's at a quarter past eight, can you imagine? And she actually has a cup of tea last thing at night, and in that part of the world "last thing at night" means about ten o'clock.'

'You've settled in all right, though?'

'I'm the blue-eyed darling; something dropped straight

out of heaven as far as Muriel Benson's concerned. She's a stupid little woman and the most crashing bore that ever existed. He's a bore, too, poor little man; well, I mean I wouldn't choose him as my ideal companion on a desert island – God, this coffee tastes good – he's actually got round to calling me "Beryl" now.'

'Has he made a pass at you?'

'Don't be silly, darling, he wouldn't know how. If he saw me naked he'd probably faint.'

'I propose to see you naked very shortly,' Vyvyan said. 'And I do assure you that one thing I won't do is to faint.'

'Nor grow weary,' Barbara said. 'At least not for some time, I hope. In a way there's something likeable about little James – but God in high heaven, what a way to conduct life. He must have swallowed a clock I think. Everything is put away and laid out in exactly the right place, everything done at exactly the right time.'

'Which is precisely how we want it. What is his routine?'

'At a quarter to nine every morning he folds up the *Daily Telegraph*, gives the fatuous Muriel something which I suppose they consider to be a kiss and goes out to the Morris 1100 in the garage. I've actually helped him to wash that car, Vyvyan; the things I've done in the course of duty!'

'He then tootles off to the bank I suppose?'

'Arriving at nine. If he's even more than five minutes out he would expect the heavens to fall. There's a sort of yard at the side of the bank —'

Vyvyan nodded. 'I know. I've seen it.'

'The little man drives in, parks his car at the back and proceeds to open up the bank.'

'And what does that consist of exactly?'

'*Exactly*, I don't know. There's a side door. He lets himself in through that; I saw him do it this morning; but precisely what goes on inside I don't know. All I know so far is that the staff don't come along until nine-thirty and that

Benson likes to have half an hour before that to "open things up" as he calls it and have a general look round.'

'I wonder how many staff there are?'

'Three men and five girls.'

'Good girl, Bar; you haven't wasted your time I can see that. What about keys?'

'All I know so far is that James has got a pretty hefty bunch of keys that he always totes around with him. Always. I should think he sleeps with them. He'd get as much fun out of them as out of that wife of his, anyway.'

'I've done a bit of prospecting too,' Vyvyan said. 'There's a coffee and bun shop called Fenners in High Parade as they call it, pretty well opposite the bank —'

'I know it.'

'I've had tea there the last three Thursdays. A strong-room van comes every Thursday afternoon between half past three and half past four. They probably vary the route a bit each time for safety reasons. It drives into that yard at the side of the bank and disappears from sight round the back. In ten minutes or so it's out again and away.

'Pretty obviously it's bringing the thirty thousand quid which Rupert Storey is going to draw out to pay his workmen the following morning.

'So every Friday morning when your little fusspot Benson lets himself into the bank to open up and start things going there's thirty thousand quid lying about and for half an hour he's alone with it.'

'So what's the next step?'

'The next step is for you to get Benson to take you with him into the bank one morning and see if you can find out what this process of "opening up" really means. Do you think you could manage that?'

'It's possible. Quite possible. James is like all men. You've only got to lay on a bit of flattery and he's wide open. But we daren't risk making him suspicious.'

'Absolutely not. *Absolutely not.* The best thing to do is

54

for you to open an account there. How much have you got in your bank here?'

'About sixty.'

'Take fifty out and open an account at Amminster.'

'And what happens to my fifty quid in the end?'

'Good grief girl. Living it up at "Wenlock" seems to have dulled your wits. Think for a moment. There are three things that can happen: (*a*) we find we can't work out a feasible scheme and the whole thing never gets off the ground in which case you kiss the Benson family good-bye, draw your fifty quid out again and we try to find some other way of doing a bit of property-distribution in our favour. Or (*b*), we think up a scheme, put it into operation and make a balls of it. In which case you and I will both land up in jug and fifty quid in a current account won't be much use to you anyway. Or finally (*c*), we pull the thing off and get away with thirty thousand quid which Rupert Storey will be expecting to pay out as wages; and if we do that what does your fifty pounds matter? It's less than a sprat to catch a bloody great big glorious fat mackerel.'

Barbara laughed. 'I rather think opening an account with James would endear me to him,' she said.

'Bound to. Bank managers like new accounts. Get into that bank with Benson one morning somehow and have a look-see. And come up to London again today fortnight.'

'If I can get the day off. You forget I'm a working woman now.'

'Drink up your coffee and come and do a bit of work for me for a nice change.'

VI

'Are you sure you don't mind, Beryl?' Muriel Benson asked. She had eventually arrived at the 'Beryl' stage, but somewhat tentatively, since she found the newcomer in the house slightly intimidating.

'You can go in with James and the library opens at half past nine, and the bus starts back from the corner of Market Street at ten minutes to ten. So you would just have time.'

'And what books shall I get for you?'

'Ask Miss Ellis. She's the Librarian. Tell her I'm in bed with this cold and I can't come in and choose for myself. She'll give you two. She knows the sort of thing I like. Are you quite sure you don't mind, now?'

Beryl said she was quite sure she didn't mind, and snatching up the two books to be returned she ran out to the garage where James Benson was already getting into the Morris.

'Good of you to do Muriel's books for her,' he said as they started off.

'I'm only too glad to. It's beastly having a fluey cold like she's got, it makes you feel absolutely rotten.'

'I hope it doesn't develop into anything worse,' James said gloomily.

Beryl laughed. 'Don't worry. We'll survive,' she said.

In discussing the strategy of her further approaches to James Benson Vyvyan had laid great stress on the importance of timing; 'choose your moment' had been his advice, 'push as hard as you like against a door when it's locked; no joy; only a little shove with it's unlatched, and you're in; Bob's your uncle'.

Beryl considered that the time had come to spring the

first of her landmines and being something of an actress she knew that she was going to enjoy herself.

'Mr Benson, I wonder if you would help me. I've been wanting to ask you for some time, only I've been a bit scared.'

'Scared of *me*? Good heavens, I'm sorry to hear that. I didn't think —'

'No, no. Not really. You're perfectly sweet to me. Only it's about money —'

'Oh – *money* —'

For a moment James thought she might be going to ask for a loan; and if she did, although he was all against lending money in principle, and wouldn't dream of doing it with anybody else, yet with Beryl —

'I've got fifty pounds.'

He was surprised; even a little startled.

'On you?'

'Yes. In my bag, here.'

'I really don't think it's wise to carry that much money about with you.'

'I know. That's why I'm asking you. I want to open an account. Is that possible?'

James Benson laughed partly in relief, partly in amusement at the simplicity of even the most sophisticated young women.

'Of course it's possible, Beryl. You mean open an account with Barrolds? I should be delighted.'

'I'm afraid it will never amount to much.'

'Don't worry about that, my dear. Little fish are sweet, that's one of the first things every bank manager learns. Do you mean you want to open it today?'

'I thought, if it suits you, I could do it this morning.'

'Of course. You can come in with me and watch me open up, if that won't bore you —'

'I'd be absolutely fascinated.

'And then I'll take your fifty pounds and we'll see to the few formalities. It's quite a painless operation.'

The car turned in from High Parade and came to rest at the back of the bank.

'Shut off from the world here,' James said. 'I always feel this is my own little kingdom.' He glanced at his watch. 'Nine o'clock on the dot. Couldn't be better. Let's see, what time does the library open?'

'Not till half past nine.'

'Splendid. That gives us plenty of time to do everything. Come along in.'

At the side door of the bank James drew out a ringful of keys attached by a long chain to a fastening inside his pocket and held them up for Beryl to see.

'The keys of the kingdom. If that sounds a bit irreverent I don't really mean it like that. It's just that being in charge of anything, even if it is only small, is a good feeling.'

'King James,' Barbara laughed. 'I suppose you never let those keys out of your sight, do you?'

'They are never off this chain and this chain is always attached pretty firmly to *me*.' James patted his prominent little stomach. 'If I ever did lose them well – I think I'd resign from the bank.'

Beryl watched him carefully as he selected one of the keys and opened the door.

As he went in the little man made a curious remark, 'Enter the Temple of Mammon.' He laughed and went on, 'That's what an Amminster character used to call us. He was a bit cracked, of course, and nobody took any notice of him. He lived in a shed somewhere out in the fields and he used to walk up and down High Parade with an old top hat on telling everyone the world was coming to an end. Outside the butcher's at the far end of the Parade he used to cry, "The slaughter of the innocents," and outside us, here, at the bank, it was always "Woe to the Temple of Mammon and all that dwell therein." '

They were in a narrow corridor now and when he had gone a few paces along it Benson stopped and reaching up pulled a handle marked 'Central Heating. Ground Floor Radiators' to the 'off' position.

Beryl was surprised as the day was decidedly chilly. Seeing the expression on her face the manager laughed, 'That's a bit of camouflage,' he said, but he didn't explain any further and he led the way into the main space of the bank, which was empty and had an odd hint of the inside of a church about it.

'The Temple of Mammon,' Beryl thought; suddenly and unexpectedly she felt scared. Vyvyan and his reassuring, cynical outlook on life seemed a long way off. The inside of the bank with the plate glass and bars in front of the cashier's position and its general air of solidity had become a frightening place suddenly and James Benson was babbling on about the local police: '... of course Amminster is only a small place and we don't have much crime, thank God; but the police here are pretty efficient all the same; if we ever did have any trouble I'm sure they would cope with it.'

'Now, my dear,' he went on, 'Would it amuse you to see the holy of holies, the strong-room: where, among other things, your fifty pounds will be quite safe.'

Rattled by her unexpected attack of nerves Beryl very nearly said 'no'. She was tempted to back out of the whole enterprise which suddenly looked formidable and frightening.

But at the back of her mind she could hear Vyvyan's scathing comments '... for Christ's sake, girl, just when it was all going our way; when you were getting it all on a plate; what the hell's the matter with you? Have you gone all moral or something? ...'

The bank manager hadn't even waited for her answer, he was leading the way along a narrow passage towards the rear and Beryl followed him until they both halted in front of a large steel door.

'That's it,' James Benson said proudly. 'The strong-room. And I don't mind telling you that every single morning when I get here I'm relieved to find that it hasn't been blown up during the night.'

'Good heavens, that isn't likely is it? You must have lots of alarms and precautions and so on, haven't you?'

Benson laughed. 'A certain number,' he agreed in a satisfied voice. 'Not as many, or as sophisticated, as at the big branches, of course, but still efficient in their way. Now, my dear, I'm going to open the strong-room door, and although I don't seriously suspect you of any criminal intent I'm afraid I can't let you watch me do it. You won't be offended, I'm sure —'

'*Of course* not,' Beryl assured him, laughing gaily and reflecting that Vyvyan, especially if in one of his black moods, would be not so much offended as hopping mad at her having got so far but not quite far enough.

'So if you don't mind waiting for a couple of minutes the other side of that door I'll go through my little ritual.'

Politely, almost apologetically, shepherded by the fussy little manager Beryl retreated a few steps back along the passage to the far side of the door.

'I'll think my evil thoughts in private here while you do whatever it is you have to do,' she said.

Benson joined in her laughter. 'It's an awful bore having to be like this with people one knows are honest,' he explained, 'but there are rules and regulations; I'm sure you understand that, my dear.'

'Absolutely,' Beryl agreed. 'All I want to do is to open my own small account.'

'Give me a couple of minutes and I'll see to it.'

James Benson pulled the door to but failed to close it entirely. A fractional slit of space ran down between the edge of the door and the jamb.

After a second's hesitation Beryl leant forward and applied her eye to this crack.

The bank manager's first action was to reach up to a red

60

button on the wall by the side of the strong-room door; an action which surprised the watching girl since beneath the button, in large red lettering, were written the words 'ALARM BELL'.

Benson kept the red button pressed home for a matter of four seconds and Beryl was even more surprised not to hear any alarm bell ringing anywhere, in fact not to hear any sound at all save her own breathing and the thumping of her heart which was beginning to beat uncomfortably fast.

Having released the 'alarm bell' Benson drew out the sacred keys again and selected a large golden-coloured one. He put this into the complicated looking lock of the strong-room door, turned it through half a circle; waited for a few seconds; then turned it again.

The heavy steel door swung open easily . . .

Beryl straightened herself up and took half a dozen quick and noiseless steps back along the passage away from the door.

A steel engraving hung on the wall and she was studying this when James Benson pushed the door open, shut and locked it behind him and rejoined her.

'Everything as it should be?' she inquired teasingly.

'Yes, everything in order, thank goodness. Everything safe and sound. As soon as I've satisfied myself about that, I'm ready to start the day. Now, what about opening that account of yours?'

Sitting in the bank manager's private office, watching James Benson fussing importantly with fountain pen, blotter and various slips of paper, Beryl found to her relief that her nerve had come back to her. Once more she was enjoying acting her role.

'I have to trouble you for three signatures.'

'No trouble,' Beryl assured him and started to write.

Almost immediately she crumpled the form up and said, 'I'm so sorry. I blotted it. Could I have another?'

The signatures being completed the question of address

arose.

'You had better put "Wenlock",' Beryl said. 'I hope to be there for some time – that is if you and Mrs Benson can put up with me.'

James Benson wrote down 'Wenlock, Amminster Green Road, Amminster', gladly.

'My dear Beryl,' he said. 'Believe me, it isn't a question of putting up with you. Your coming to "Wenlock" has been the nicest thing that has happened to us, and if you will let me say so to me personally, for a very long time.'

At the library Miss Ellis, like the good small-town librarian that she was, knew all about Muriel Benson's likes and dislikes.

'Sorry to hear Mrs Benson isn't well,' she said. 'She's usually so bright and cheerful. I've got the latest Jean Plaidy on one side for her. I know she'll enjoy that. And I'll look out a good detective story.'

'Is Mrs Benson fond of detective stories, then?'

'She reads every one I can get hold of for her. Funny, isn't it, all this interest in crime? There's too much crime about if you ask me.'

'Much too much,' Beryl agreed piously.

Muriel Benson completely recovered from her cold and was her usual bustling cheerful self again in time for the children's gymkhana.

This was an annual event in Amminster and was held in the Rectory Field about half a mile out of the town.

The two children, Ursula and Penny, were bitten with the small-girl bug of horse worship and under Beryl's direction had been practising assiduously for their two events.

In her day Beryl had herself gone through a similar phase of horse madness and she enjoyed the afternoons with the two girls and Polly in the field at the back of the house.

The girls naturally regarded Polly as being of unsurpassed, and indeed unsurpassable, excellence; but con-

62

sidered through more sober eyes she was a flea-bitten, aged pony with a dippy back, having pleasant enough manners but of very ordinary performance.

Ursula was to ride her in the Bending Race and later Penny in the Musical Chairs; and although neither of the girls really expected to win her event, Muriel Benson, with the incurable optimism of a mother, nursed secret hopes that one of them might.

The gymkhana afternoon followed the traditional course of such things. First came the jumping, in which Polly did not compete; then the Bending Race, run in two heats and final. Ursula actually won her heat, this causing great excitement in the Benson camp, but in the final she was not only unplaced but actually fell off and ended up in tears.

The Sack Race and the Egg and Spoon Race gave an opportunity for opening the picnic basket for tea and finally came the Musical Chairs in which Penny, an intelligent and hardy little rider, was only just beaten and so won a consolation prize.

A large number of people came to the event not only from Amminster but from a wide circle round and the ring was completely encircled in cars.

After the last event the Benson party started back for 'Wenlock' on foot: Penny riding Polly, Ursula leading the pony, Muriel Benson and Beryl behind.

As they were leaving the Rectory Field an open sports car went by on the road. A bare-headed, good-looking young man was driving; a dark-haired girl sat by his side; and a similar young couple were behind.

The young man at the wheel was busy talking and laughing with his companion and when he first caught sight of Beryl what he saw didn't register for the moment.

Then he gave a quick, surprised, backward glance and shot a hand into the air in salute.

' 'Lo, Barbara,' he called. 'What brings you here?'

Luckily the flow of traffic was already taking the sports car out of earshot and the situation didn't develop. There was a good deal of chatter and noise going on all round and Beryl couldn't be certain how much the incident had registered with Muriel Benson.

Not much she devoutly hoped. Freddie Le Neve Trench, welcome though he had been at one time as a cheerful escort round the West End, was the last person she wanted to see in the present circumstances.

Polly took exception to some road repairs which were going on and had to be coaxed past them so it was quite a few moments before Muriel Benson asked, 'Didn't that young man in the car call you *Barbara*?'

Beryl laughed easily.

'Freddie? Yes, he did. He always used to call me Barbara. Actually' (even as she was talking she was agreeably surprised at the ease with which she could invent lies and the fluency with which she could utter them) 'actually it's my second name. I was christened Beryl Barbara, but I never liked it and don't use it. But when I was going about with Freddie he said it was one of his favourite names and he always used to call me by it.'

'I suppose you were very friendly with him at one time, were you?'

'With Freddie? We did have a bit of a whirl together, yes.'

'He looked awfully nice. Were you very fond of him, Beryl?'

'He was always a gay spark. Yes, I was fond of him, I suppose.'

'Oh dear —' Muriel Benson said, but mostly to herself. She scented a broken romance and she was intrigued by it.

That evening when she and James were alone in the living-room of 'Wenlock' she recounted all the happenings of the afternoon and said, 'I was quite right, you see, about

64

Beryl coming here to get over a love affair. I'm sure I was. What a pity; he looked such a nice young man too.'

'I'm sure Beryl only has nice friends,' James said. 'She's a very nice young person.'

Barbara was stretched full length luxuriating in a bath as hot as she could bear it. The water was a vivid green, coloured by the pine essence she had poured into it. The nipples of her firm, shapely breasts made two small coral islets above that green sea.

She heard the front door open and shut. A moment later Vyvyan, realising that somebody else was in the flat, called out:

'Is that you, Bar? Are you in there?'

'Who the hell do you think it is?' Barbara called back amiably. 'Have you got some other woman knocking about?'

'I'll be in in a moment.'

A minute or two later he came into the tiny bathroom carrying two glasses of champagne.

'Champers in the bath!' Barbara said. 'What a splendid idea. What are we celebrating?'

'It's one of the few we've got left so we might as well open it. I walked out of T.M. & F. for good this afternoon.'

'I thought you were there for another three months?'

'Not with that sarcastic bastard Fitzwarren. I've just about had a bellyful of him.'

'So now what's the magnificent income that we are supposed to live on?'

'Sweet Fanny Adams,' Vyvyan smiled his attractive dark smile and raised his glass. 'Cheers, darling. Here's to naked women in sea-green water. A very fetching combination of colours. Sweet Fanny Adams at the moment; but not to worry. There's plenty of money knocking about in the world and you and I are going to do a little redistribution of it presently.'

Barbara sipped her champagne and Vyvyan watched her hungrily.

'Don't be long,' he said, 'and we can talk afterwards.'

Afterwards they did talk; lying side by side on the divan bed; smoking cigarettes of satisfied content; looking up at the ceiling.

'What's the news from the Amminster front?' Vyvyan asked. Barbara had a lot to tell him, but she proposed to tell it in her own way.

'Do you remember Freddie Le Neve Trench?' she asked.

'The Young Guardee? Who's he poking now?'

'Don't be coarse. And anyway I don't think you are in any position at the moment to reprimand anybody for that particular activity. Freddie was at the Amminster Gymkhana.'

'The devil he was. Did he see you?'

'Only right at the end. As he was whirling by in his M.G. He did call out "Barbara" though; and Mrs Benson heard him.

'Did she say anything?'

'I put her off with a story about it being my second name and how Freddie always used to call me by it and so on. I rather think she suspects a shattered romance. She's ready to see a Denise Robins situation in everything. Also, incidentally, she's keen on detective stories.'

'The deuce she is. What about that account of yours?'

'I've opened it. James took me into the bank with him last Wednesday morning.'

'Tell me. Everything. Slowly.'

Barbara told him everything, slowly. Vyvyan listened to her in concentrated attention.

'... just for a moment, when we first got inside, I was scared. No tummy feeling; Christ, I thought, I must be mad to be getting mixed up in a thing like this ... *things can go wrong ...*'

'Let's go over it all again slowly,' Vyvyan said, 'and try to make sure things don't go wrong.'

Barbara went over it all again, slowly; and Vyvyan picked up her account point by point.

He started by saying, 'T.M. & F. used to handle advertising for Rocks, the safe and security people. The character I used to deal with there, a chap called Dan Vandenberg, has left them. There was some sort of row; I think he was hopping into young Mrs Rock's bed, I'm not sure; but I ran across him at Sandown Park not long ago and I've been seeing quite a bit of him lately.'

'I hope you didn't ask him the best way to break open a safe?'

'Darling, if you ask damn fool questions like that I shall rouse myself out of a very pleasant lethargy, turn you over and spank you really hard where it hurts.'

'You do make some splendid suggestions.'

Vyvyan ignored the invitation.

'Of course I was more than careful what I said,' he went on, 'but Dan is the sort of chap who likes showing off how much he knows and it was possible to pick up quite a few ideas that might be useful.

'That business of pulling off the switch marked Central Heating as soon as you get into the bank, for instance.'

'James Benson called it a bit of camouflage.'

'Which tells us all we want to know about it. It's all Lombard Street to a china orange that that's the switch for the alarm bell. Central Heating my foot. That switch gets pulled into the "on" position by whoever leaves the bank last every evening and once it's "on" you can't open a door inside the place, or any of the windows, and probably not even touch the strong-room without setting off an alarm in the local H.Q. of the law and having a couple of police cars buzzing round in no time at all flat.

'So, of course, the first thing your little man James does when he gets in the place is to put it off. Which is precisely what we shall do, too.

'Tell me again about what you saw of the strong-room door —'

He listened with intense concentration to Barbara's slowly repeated account, and then said, 'Same thing there: a thousand to one it's the same thing. There almost certainly *will* be an alarm bellpush somewhere, but it will be hidden. The thing marked "Alarm Bell" must be some sort of electric control connected with the lock on the strong-room door. You say Benson kept it pressed in for a second or two?'

'Quite noticeably. A good four seconds I'd say.'

Vyvyan nodded. 'And the key?'

'He turned it through a half circle. Then waited. I'd say three seconds at least. Then turned it again.'

Vyvyan smiled slowly in satisfaction.

'You're earning your keep, Bar, I'll say that for you.'

'As long as the keep comes. And plenty of it.'

'Thirty thousand seems plenty to me. I'm not greedy. Just an ardent Distributivist. Thirty thousand less fifty actually. How did opening your account go?'

'I nearly made a boob there.'

'A boob?' Vyvyan's voice hardened and sharpened suddenly. 'What happened?'

'I had to give three specimen signatures.'

'Well, of course you did. That's normal practice. If they don't have three signatures they can't feed mistakes into the computer.'

'Yes. But I wrote down my own name, in the proper way. Barbara Courlander.'

'What a bloody silly thing to do.'

'Of course it was. But damn it, Vyvyan, don't be so superior about it. If you are suddenly asked to sign something – you do it in the usual way. It's automatic.'

Vyvyan nodded reluctantly.

'Did Benson notice?' he asked.

'He couldn't possibly have done. I simply said I had

made a blot on the form and asked for another one.'

'What did you do with the first one?'

'Scrumpled it up.'

'And?'

'Threw it into the wastepaper basket.'

'Which wasn't very wise either.'

'You don't seriously believe that James Benson is going through the contents of all the wastepaper baskets in the bank?'

'Probably not. No. And anyway it's done now. But the sooner we have a shot at this thing now the better. I've been down at Amminster two days this week making a final recce.' He stubbed out his cigarette in the glass ashtray on the bedside table. 'Let's get up and put some clothes on and while you're making a pot of coffee I'll get out the map.'

Five minutes later Barbara was looking with lively interest at an ordnance sheet spread out on the table.

'What a marvellous map. It shows absolutely everything.'

'It's a six-inch ordnance,' Vyvyan explained, 'so there isn't much it misses. This is where you are —' He pointed with his finger and Barbara nodded.

'And this is the main road into Amminster along which your little fusspot James Benson drives himself every day. Now, pretty well halfway between his house and the beginning of Amminster there's a turning to the right, here —'

'I know it. I've taken the children along it with the pony. It isn't much of a road; it doesn't lead anywhere. Hardly anybody uses it.'

'Which is exactly why it suits us. Now listen carefully, Bar. I've worked this thing out and I think I've got a good plan. But we aren't committed to it yet, and if any points come up that you don't like as we talk it over we can see if they need revision.

'The first thing you've got to do when you go back is to spin a yarn about some family event – wedding, funeral, christening, it doesn't matter very much what you make it;

a funeral's best probably because of the short notice.

'Your spiel is that you have simply got to attend this thing which will entail being away for the night. Your brother is taking you to it and will call for you round about nine on Friday morning.

'Can you find an excuse for being out of the house before breakfast that morning without arousing any suspicion?'

'Easily. I often go out for ten minutes before breakfast and have a look at Polly in the field.'

'Good. But never mind about Polly in the field. Get into the garage and hamstring that car of Benson's – what sort is it?'

'A Morris 1100.'

'Right. The best way to deal with it is to disconnect the high-tension lead, just under the bonnet. I'll give you some lessons in doing that on my bus.'

'No need to. I had an 1100 once.'

'All the same we'll practise it a couple of times. Then you go into breakfast in the normal way and when James Benson comes out at ten to nine to set off for the bank you come out with him to see him off. O.K.?'

'Perfectly, so far. There won't be anything unusual about any of that.'

'Benson gets into his Morris and switches on. No joy. Is he anything of a mechanic by the way?'

'He hasn't a clue about what makes a car go. Any trouble of any sort and he rings up the garage in Amminster.'

'Good. At that precise point in time I appear on the scene in my Volvo which I'll keep as much out of sight as possible. 'Oh, how lucky, Mr Benson,' you exclaim. 'Here's my brother come to pick me up! We can give you a lift to the bank and you can telephone the garage from there.' My guess is he'll fall for it; yes?'

Barbara gave an excited little laugh. 'He's absolutely certain to,' she agreed. 'If he was half an hour late opening up the bank James would think he had committed some sort of mortal sin.'

'Exactly. We all pile into the Volvo, you with your suitcase of course. And don't forget you'll have to pack everything in it. You mustn't leave anything behind. Benson will be in the front passenger's seat and you'll be at the back.

'Halfway to Amminster, just as he's telling us for the third time how kind it is, etc. I turn right along that road we were looking at on the map.

'Your little James gets agitated, "I think you're going the wrong way"—'

'That will be where you press the muzzle of the gun against the back of his neck. Hard.'

'The gun?'

'And it will be my cue for saying, "Just keep absolutely quiet, Benson, and do exactly as you're told and you won't get hurt. Step out of line in any way and you'll have a hole blown out of the back of your head as big as a soup plate." I think he'll be scared.'

'The poor little man will wet his pants he'll be so scared,' Barbara said, 'but a gun – I didn't realise there was going to be a gun.'

'How else are we going to scare him? But don't worry. I'm scared of guns, too. And I've no intention of having the genuine article; that would only get us into much worse trouble if we got caught. What we want is something that looks and feels exactly like a pistol, but is really a dummy. A theatrical thing. Can't you get one from that Antique place where you used to work?'

'Tooveys? Yes, I expect I could.'

'Say you want it for an amateur theatrical show you're putting on, or acting in, or whatever.'

Barbara nodded.

'Half a mile along the turning that leads nowhere the ground falls away at the side of the road. There's a hollow there, like a cave almost. That's where we stop the Volvo; tie Benson up and gag him – I'll have scarves and so on in the back of the car – tip him out and roll him into the gorse and undergrowth of this cave place.

'Having first of all of course taken his keys. I'll bring a pair of pliers along to cut the chain if we can't pull it off him.

'Then you and I will get back into the Volvo, go like the clappers into Amminster and try our luck in opening up the bank instead of Benson.

'We may find snags there that we don't know anything about, if that happens we beat it and get to hell out of things as fast as possible.

'If we're lucky and things go right we beat it just the same and get to hell away from Amminster as fast as possible; but this time with a couple of sacks stuffed with thirty thousand quid in the back of the car.'

VII

Friday morning was crisp and dry and sunny.

'Beryl will have a lovely week-end,' Muriel Benson thought. 'I'm so glad.'

At twenty minutes to nine it was time for James Benson to glance at the clock, push his cup across the table and say, 'I've just got time for my second, I think.'

He duly glanced at the clock, pushed his cup forward and said it.

His wife would have thought that something was wrong if all these minutiae had not happened in precisely that sequence, at precisely that time.

She poured out her husband's 'second' and was handing the cup back to him as Beryl came into the room.

Beryl had already had her meagre breakfast – a token affair only – and had been out to the field to see that Polly was all right.

This was normal procedure with her and Muriel Benson automatically asked the normal question, 'Is the pony all right?'

'Absolutely,' Beryl assured her. 'In great form. As soon as I'm back from the week-end I must really get down to exercising her a bit more.'

'Those two lazy girls ought to be up and out with you,' Muriel said.

'Oh well, I expect they'll be down soon enough,' Beryl answered indulgently. Actually what she hoped was that the girls wouldn't be down too soon. This was one morning when her early excursion from the house had not been to look over the gate into the field, but to the garage instead.

She knew that there was not the slightest chance of being

seen by either James or Muriel Benson, both of whom were immersed in the routine of breakfast; but as she had been coming out of the garage she had glanced up and there was Penny looking through the window of the girls' bedroom.

The child had waved and Beryl had waved back. No harm done so far. But if Penny got dressed in time and came downstairs full of curiosity about 'What were you doing in the garage, Beryl?' it might prove awkward ...

James drained his second cup of tea; glanced at the clock again; dabbed his lips with his napkin and uttered the invariable remark which by now Beryl knew by heart, 'Well, mustn't keep Mr Barrold waiting, I suppose.'

He rose, gave his wife the prim little peck of passionless custom and went out into the hall. Beryl following him.

Friday was invariably a full day at the bank, and James was always relieved when mid-morning came and the big transaction of cash for Storey's was safely over. Even in a sleepy place like Amminster Storey's brought pretty imposing safeguards along for the collection of the money and James didn't really expect any trouble, but nevertheless it was always a relief to get back to 'Wenlock' just after six on a Friday evening and know that everything had once more gone off uneventfully ...

On the way to the garage he spoke to Beryl about her coming week-end.

'What time is your brother coming for you?' he asked.

'Any time now. He said about nine or just before. But I don't suppose he'll be as punctual as you, Mr Benson.'

James Benson gave a chuckle of great self-content.

'And where is it you are off to?' he inquired.

'To this funeral I told you about and then to see our parents in Lincolnshire. I'm afraid I don't get to see them nowadays as often as I should.'

'I'm sure they are lucky to have a daughter like you,' James said, and for a fleeting instant Beryl found herself feeling just a little bit mean.

74

James got into his Morris 1100.

'I expect you've arranged with Mrs Benson when you'll be back?' he said, lowering the window.

'Sunday evening,' Beryl lied cheerfully.

James nodded. 'Have a good time then,' he said, and turned the starting key.

Nothing happened.

He tried again. Still nothing.

'She usually starts like a bird,' he said. 'I wonder what's wrong?'

'Try again,' Beryl advised. 'I expect the engine's a bit cold.'

'It has never minded the cold before,' James said, and tried again.

And again; and again; and again . . .

Even to totally unmechanical ears like his it became increasingly clear that for some reason or other the engine was without life.

Mechanically this was not surprising since the H.T. lead was disconnected from its terminal.

James began to get agitated.

'I'll have to ring Wilson's garage,' he said, 'and ask them to send a taxi out. Let's hope they have one on hand, or I shall be really hideously late.'

A horn blared from the end of the drive and Beryl gave a cry of well-simulated surprise.

'That's my brother in the Volvo,' she said. 'How marvellously lucky. He's just in time. We can run you down to the bank, Mr Benson, and you can ring up the garage from there.'

'Could you really?'

'Of course. You won't be late at all. Don't worry.'

'It's very kind of you —'

Beryl was already beginning to carry her case towards the gate.

James insisted on carrying it for her and was surprised by

its weight.

'Good heavens, you girls do take a lot away just for the week-end,' he said.

Beryl laughed easily. 'I'm afraid we are vain creatures,' she said; she was slightly disturbed by his remark, but correctly guessed that the little man would be too relieved at finding that he wasn't going to be late after all to worry much about any details.

When they reached the Volvo she said, 'Mr Benson, this is my brother Vincent. Vincent, we can give Mr Benson a lift into Amminster, can't we?'

'Of course we can. Delighted.'

'His car won't start for some reason.'

'Would you like me to have a look at it for you, Mr Benson?'

'No, please, don't do that. The garage can send a man out during the day. It's a question of time now. I really must be down at the bank by nine, or a minute or two after.'

'Hop in. We'll have you there in a brace of shakes.'

Beryl had already installed herself and her case in the back. James Benson gratefully got into the passenger's seat in front.

'All aboard?' Vyvyan asked cheerfully and turned the starting key. The engine sprang into life immediately and the Volvo moved off.

'I must say this is extremely fortunate,' James said in great good content. 'I don't think I shall be more than five minutes late.'

'You won't be that if I can help it,' Vyvyan assured him. 'I'll make up time for you. These cars can travel.'

'As long as we don't have an accident *en route*,' James said, laughing a trifle nervously.

'Keep your fingers crossed.'

There was no more than the usual thin early morning traffic and fulfilling Vyvyan's promise in the matter the

Volvo certainly did travel.

So fast, indeed, that the car had swung off the main road before James collected wits and breath to expostulate, 'Mr Carpenter, we're going the wrong way —'

From that moment James Benson's world collapsed terrifyingly about him.

Something very hard and very cold was pressed against the base of his skull and the girl he had known as Beryl Carpenter said in a voice he only just recognised, 'Don't shout, or try anything funny, or I'll blow your head off.'

VIII

By a quarter to eleven the Volvo was parked in its usual place half on the roadway, half on the pavement of Hambledon Street; and the living-room of the flat presented an extraordinary sight.

'I make it seven hundred tenners,' Vyvyan announced, 'two thousand fivers, and just over ten thousand ones. Twenty-seven thousand plus.'

'A bit better than what you used to bring back from T.M. & W.,' Barbara said. Her dark eyes were brilliant with excitement.

'I wonder what Rupert Storey will use for wages today.'

Barbara laughed. 'That's his look-out. Do you think someone has found James Benson by now?'

Vyvyan glanced at his wrist-watch and said, 'I hope so. We don't want the poor little devil to come to any real harm.'

Barbara laughed again. 'By God, he was scared,' she said. 'I told you he would just about wet his pants with fright and I should think he probably did.'

Vyvyan looked at her curiously.

'You enjoyed it, didn't you?' he asked.

The girl nodded. 'Yes, I did. When I had that gun in my hand, pressing it against the back of his neck, of course it wasn't a real one but he didn't know that – I felt, I felt as though I wished it *had* been real.'

'The female of the species,' Vyvyan said. 'Well, the first thing is to get this lot stashed away as we arranged, so let's start.'

The question of the best hiding-place for the money had been a matter of prolonged discussion between them. Barbara had made a number of ingenious suggestions, but Vyvyan judged them too ingenious.

'There's no point in trying to be clever about it,' he said. 'All we want to do is to make sure the ordinary visitor to the flat doesn't see the stuff. If the police do get on to us and come to search the place believe me they'll go through it with a fine toothcomb. They'll unpick the mattresses and have the floorboards up – the lot.'

Barbara supposed there was sense in this and in the end somewhat reluctantly agreed to Vyvyan's plan that four suitcases – two of her own together with a large Rev-robe and a case of Vyvyan's – should be used as a cache for the stolen notes.

It didn't take long, now, to put this plan into operation and before half past eleven the money was put into the cases and the cases themselves safely stowed away in the 'glory-hole', a place which in more spacious days, before the house had been cut up into flats, had presumably been a housemaid's pantry and which was still, conveniently, furnished with a door.

Having put the now filled cases away Vyvyan shut the glory-hole door, locked it and slipped the key into his pocket.

Barbara watched him and asked, 'And when do we start using it?'

'Not yet. The notes aren't new, thank goodness, so I can't see that there's much danger of their being traced. But we'll play it safe. With the amount of stuff being stolen today if we give it six months we ought to be absolutely in the clear.'

'I wonder what's happening at Amminster?'

'I expect the C.I.D. down there are buzzing about like flies. We really deserve a vote of thanks for giving them something to do.'

'Twenty-seven thousand pounds! It was a marvellous idea of yours, Vyvyan.'

'A small case of redistribution of property.'

Barbara laughed. 'If that's what you call it,' she said.

'And you did your part wonderfully.'

'I enjoyed every second of it – especially the bit in the car. I wonder if there'll be anything on the radio about it.'

'We'll put the one o'clock news on and see.'

'Then we'll go out to the Pot and celebrate. I'm in the mood for celebrating, Vyvyan. I had no idea it would make me feel like this – all excited and keyed up.'

'Let's just be sure we've got all the details tidied up first. Where's the gun?'

'You brought it in from the car, didn't you?'

'*I* didn't. I thought you did.'

They stared at one another until eventually Barbara forced an unconvincing laugh and said, 'Well, it must be in the Volvo then, mustn't it?'

'By God, it had better be,' Vyvyan answered, and they went out to look.

It took less than a minute to go out of the flat and along the few yards of pavement to where the Volvo was parked.

In those sixty seconds Vyvyan first of all knew for certain that the gun would be somewhere in the car – fallen on to the floor probably, or slipped down the crack behind the back seat; this certitude was instantly followed by an equally strong conviction that something had gone wrong and it wouldn't be there, and for a moment he felt uncomfortably cold in the pit of his stomach.

'It's got to be there,' he told himself as he drew out his keys and unlocked the car door, 'it's got to be.'

The gun wasn't there.

Actually a minute was enough to convince them of the fact; and after five minutes of repetitive, inch by inch searching there was no point in hoping any longer.

They stood on the pavement of Hambledon Street looking so blankly at one another that a casual passer-by inquired facetiously, 'Lost something, mate?'

The query jolted Vyvyan. The hard, cold ball had come into his stomach again and he felt a little sick.

He jerked his head to indicate the house and without speaking they both went back into the flat.

Inside the living-room Vyvyan shut the door behind him and leaned against it.

'God Almighty,' he said. 'What a mess.'

Barbara astonished him by laughing.

'What in hell happened to the gun?' Vyvyan demanded.

'There's only one thing that can have happened to it. When we started tying Benson up I suppose I put it down on the seat —'

'You suppose!'

'How could I have helped you with tying him up and gagging him if I hadn't put it down?'

Vyvyan stared at her and said, 'Christ, I simply clean forgot about the gun. As soon as everything started and it was all going as we planned I clean forgot about it.'

'When we were bundling him out of the car and rolling him down that bank we must have swept the gun out as well without realising it.'

Vyvyan considered this for a few seconds and then nodded slowly.

'That's about the size of it. Must be.'

Barbara laughed again.

'But we've still got the money,' she said. 'Twenty-seven thousand pounds of it.'

'And the police have got the gun.'

'If they find it. They won't be looking for a gun. Nobody's been shot.'

'They'll find it.'

Barbara crossed to the drinks table and mixed herself a generous gin and tonic.

'One for you?' she asked.

Vyvyan joined her and poured Scotch into a tumbler.

'On the strong side, isn't it?' Barbara asked.

'I want a strong one. God, to think we could make a mess of it like this. This is just what I told them all months ago didn't have to be made – the one silly mistake. You think it all out, plan everything and then when you are actually doing the thing, when it's happening —' He shook his head and threw up his hands in a gesture of despair.

'Even supposing they do find it,' Barbara said. 'How are they going to tell where it was bought? There must be hundreds, thousands probably, of these dummy things up and down England, how are they going to know where this one particular one came from? How are they going to trace it to Tooveys?'

Vyvyan listened to her. He wanted to be convinced.

'Weren't the things in Tooveys marked in some way to show where they came from, then?'

'No. Of course they weren't. Just a price tag, that's all; and that was taken off when the article was sold.'

'And you think there are lots of these dummy pistols about?'

'How many amateur theatrical companies are there up and down the country? Ten thousand? More I should think. And I expect at least half of them have got a dummy gun among their props.'

'You're a lot cooler about it than I am.'

Barbara shook her head.

'I'm not cool at all. Not one bit. I'm boiling with excitement. It's the most exciting thing that's ever happened to me. I'd do it all again tomorrow for the thrill of it. We've got away with twenty-seven thousand pounds and we aren't going to be caught.'

'We hope.'

'I know we're not.'

Vyvyan drained his glass. 'We'll see what the one o'clock news has to say about it,' he said.

The one o'clock news programme was largely over-shadowed by the kidnapping of a Foreign Office official on a courtesy visit to one of the South America republics, against which a mere twenty-seven thousand-pound bank robbery didn't rate very highly.

The Amminster affair was mentioned, but the only hard facts to emerge so far were that Barrolds bank there had, indeed, been robbed and that the trussed-up bank manager had been discovered and, beyond a certain amount of shock, was none the worse for his experience.

'Thank God for that,' Vyvyan said when it was obvious that no more news would be forthcoming. 'I was afraid the pompous little fool might have suffocated, or had a heart attack, or something.'

'You're determined to be pessimistic about it. And please note, nothing has been said about the gun.'

'It can't possibly still be somewhere in the car, can it?'

'No. Of course it can't,' Barbara said sharply. 'We know that. We've searched every inch of the Volvo. When we moved James Benson out of the car the gun must have gone with him somehow. So it's in that tangle of undergrowth and bracken by the side of the road and with a bit of luck it will stay there.'

At six o'clock when Vyvyan was setting out on his usual visit to the corner shop to get the evening paper Barbara called after him, 'Get the *News* as well as the *Standard*.'

He turned back into the room and said a little doubtfully, 'I wonder if it's wise —'

'Oh for God's sake,' Barbara burst out. 'Why shouldn't we have two evening papers if we want them? How can your asking one evening for the *News* as well as the *Standard* possibly be tied up with a bank robbery down at Amminster? I keep telling you, Vyvyan, we've done the job just as we said we would and we're away, clear. If you go creeping about looking as though you expect to be suspected people will begin to get suspicious. We've got twenty-seven thousand pounds to blue, so let's blue it and enjoy ourselves and to hell with everybody.'

Both *Standard* and *News* gave up their front page to the kidnapped F.O. official, but the Amminster bank robbery got reasonably full treatment on the inside pages, particularly in the *Standard* which seized on the au pair aspect of the story and seemed willing to open up a correspondence on the theme of 'How safe is the au pair in your home?'

Bank manager, James Benson, had been treated at the Amminster and District General Hospital for shock and had then been allowed to go home.

An enterprising reporter had managed to interview Mrs Benson who said, 'Beryl was such a thoroughly nice girl I simply cannot believe that she really had a hand in it. She must have been under some evil influence.'

Barbara laughed when she read it.

'That's you,' she pointed out. 'You're my evil influence.'

But Vyvyan was already beginning to feel that the exact opposite was the case.

Boredom, half sardonic half amused, at the sterile futility of life as he saw it lived around him in his London set had led him first of all to argue about the possibility of the successful crime, and then to give himself the curious exercise of seeing whether he could plot one in detail.

While actually carrying out the robbery there had been moments of excitement which were undeniably enjoyable; but they had been due to the heat of action and the immediate presence of danger. All immediacy had gone now. He had got the money and in time he meant to enjoy it; but meanwhile all excitement and enjoyment had vanished.

But obviously not for Barbara.

It was as though she had taken the first sip of a drug which had laid strong hold on her.

During the next few weeks Vyvyan would have been pleased to let all reference to Amminster drop; but Barbara would not, apparently could not, let the matter alone, going back constantly over every detail of the car ride into the town and the events in the bank.

She was genuinely disappointed by the rapidity with which all reference to the affair got squeezed out of the papers by larger violences from various parts of the world.

The 'Is your au pair a danger?' correspondence fizzled out unexpectedly, and the editorial curtain was rung down with the conventional statement that the police were 'working on several lines of inquiry'.

'I wonder what that means,' Vyvyan said.

'Nothing. They've got nothing to work on. If they had found the gun they would have said so. We've got the lovely money, and we'll start spending it soon.'

IX

Detective Inspector William Lawson got out of the official car outside the front door of 'Wenlock' and told the driver to wait.

'I shouldn't be long,' he said. 'I'm not really expecting to get anything.' Then, ending on the eternal note of irrational optimism which every C.I.D. man must possess or go mad, he added cheerfully, 'But you never know.'

The policeman driver smiled and nodded. 'Good luck, sir,' he said.

Allowing for the fact that everybody in authority had to be looked at slightly askance the driver liked the inspector.

William Lawson expected his team to work hard, but he worked hard himself and he treated his men fairly.

He was a well-built, burly man of forty-eight. He was beginning to put on weight but the sinew and muscle which had served him well in the boxing ring and on the rugger field were still there and if ever he got involved in a personal affray he was still a formidable opponent.

Lawson had become a policeman because as a young man the life appealed to him. He had thought of it then as something of a vocation and a fine career. Now, thirty years later, he was lucky enough still to have the same feelings.

In his climb up the ladder to his present position of inspector he had experienced the inevitable periods of frustration and disillusionment; but they had soon passed, and on the whole he could look back on his career and declare that he was a satisfied man.

He had been at Amminster a long time now and there wasn't much he didn't know about the local villains.

They all knew him, of course, and not a few of the old

professionals among them were willing to give him some degree of grudging respect for playing the game hard but fairly.

In his time at Amminster the inspector had dealt with a murder; several cases of g.b.h.; a number of breakings-in, and of course hundreds of minor matters; but as far as actual robbery went the Barrolds bank affair was the biggest thing that had come his way.

By chance he had been in the station shortly after nine-thirty on the Friday morning when the alarm came through from the bank.

Intense activity was immediately set in motion, two police cars being sent to the bank itself and a third up to 'Wenlock'.

At ten-forty the bank manager, James Benson, was brought into the station by a farmer called Enoch Lacey.

Benson was scared and in a state of semi-shock, but he was able to give an account of what had happened to him – in fact, he couldn't be stopped from continually repeating his rather incoherent tale – and he was finally driven out in the inspector's car to indicate exactly where the attack on him had taken place.

When eventually the bank manager's story was put into intelligent shape Lawson, having set all the machinery he could in motion, sat down to study it in detail.

Benson had been half pulled, half pushed out of the car; then, gagged and bound, had been jostled and rolled down the steep bank at the side of the road till he finally came to rest on a ledge which formed a sort of cave, so overgrown by bracken and rough grass as to be almost hidden.

He lay there for some time expecting any moment, he said, to have a heart attack.

'I was absolutely stunned by it all, Inspector. Well, I suppose the truth is I was scared to death.'

'Don't worry, Mr Benson. Most people would have been.'

'I just couldn't think, or do anything for a bit. What with the gag thing in my mouth and my heart thumping I honestly thought I'd had it. I thought I was going to pass out.'

'Did you faint in fact?'

'No, I didn't. Not quite. After a bit my heart seemed to slow down and I managed to breathe a bit more easily, and I thought: no good just lying here like this. I've got to do something.'

'So what did you do?'

'You understand of course that my legs were tied at the ankles and my wrists behind my back so there wasn't a lot I could do really; but I worked my way to the edge of this sort of shelf I was lying on and then actually without meaning it I rolled out and went turning and tumbling down the bank right to the bottom.

'I had to lie there for a while because coming bumping down like that shook me up and my heart started to thump again; but I found that scraping down the bank had loosened the scarf they had tied my ankles with a little and I could move my legs more.

'What I wanted to do was to get up to the top of the bank again on to the road, but I didn't think I'd ever make it, so I started to crawl along where I was on the level.

'I didn't know where I was heading for, but it seemed better than just lying there and then after a few minutes I heard a tractor . . .'

Enoch Lacey had been the driver of the tractor. Lacey was a taciturn man who farmed, mainly in the market-garden line, on the outskirts of the town.

He had untied and ungagged Benson, taken him back to the ramshackle farmhouse (where the bank manager all but collapsed) and eventually had brought him in to the police station.

Both James Benson and his wife had, of course, been intensively interviewed and questioned. A vast number of words had been spoken, especially by Muriel Benson, and up to a point Lawson had been able to get a lot of information; that is to say he had been given a description, almost photographic in its detail, of what the girl in the case looked like.

Muriel Benson kept interleaving her voluble comments with professions of incredulity.

'I simply cannot believe it, Mr Lawson; I *cannot* believe it; she seemed such a lady —'

'All sorts of people turn villain these days, Mrs Benson.'

'But she seemed so *nice*; so — you know what I mean. I can't believe it.'

'I'm afraid you've got to believe it,' the inspector told her a little forcibly ...

Muriel Benson had no objection to the inspector paying her yet another visit, and she went through the traditional routine of making him welcome and suggesting, almost insisting on, a cup of tea.

Lawson didn't want the tea; but he wouldn't have dreamt of refusing it. Long experience had taught him that your cup of tea is a great loosener of tongues and jogger of memories.

'Hope you don't mind my troubling you again, Mrs Benson —' he began.

Muriel Benson didn't mind in the slightest, she enjoyed it.

'I know I've been over it all with you half a dozen times already; but I'm afraid it's the only way: keep on talking about it and asking questions and in the end something turns up' ('*we hope*' he added under his breath because, despite a cheerful exterior, the inspector was beginning to fear that nothing worth calling a clue was ever going to make an appearance in the case).

'Now, the only letter you had from this woman was in reply to the advertisement in the local paper – is that right?'

Muriel Benson nodded.

'And there wasn't any address on it?'

'No; I don't think so. I'm sure there wasn't. All it said was, "with reference to the suggested post could we meet at Fenners coffee shop and talk it over" – if those weren't the exact words, it was something very much like that.'

'And you didn't notice the postmark?'

'I'm afraid not. I'd know her writing again though, at once.'

'Distinctive was it?'

'Very. It was characterful writing. Strong. It was what I call a lady's hand, Inspector.'

'And all the time she was with you this Miss Carpenter never received a letter from anybody?'

'I don't think she did.'

'Didn't that strike you as a little odd?'

'Well, once or twice I was just a shade curious about her. I thought perhaps she had had a broken love affair and was hiding away from people. And, of course, her father being an out-of-the-world clergyman somewhere in Lincolnshire —'

'There isn't a parson of the name of Carpenter in Lincolnshire who knows a thing about her,' the inspector said. 'We've checked that.'

'I'm afraid she didn't tell the truth,' Muriel Benson sighed.

'I'm afraid she didn't,' Lawson agreed grimly. He laid the book he had been nursing on the table and said, 'I've got a few more photographs here of women who work with men in the confidence trick line. See if you can spot her.'

Mrs Benson turned over the pages slowly, fascinated by the full face and left and right profile pictures of a couple of dozen women.

Most of them were good-lookers in a hard brassy way; it wasn't difficult to imagine the bright yellow hair darkening at the roots, the brilliantly painted nails.

Finally she shut the book and shook her head.

'She's not there,' she said.

Lawson wasn't unduly disappointed; he hadn't really had any great hopes.

'I'd like to go just once more over the events of the Friday morning,' he said, 'the day it happened —'

Muriel Benson nodded brightly.

'First of all, had there been anything unusual in the few days immediately before that Friday? Any telephone calls for instance?'

'I can't remember that she ever had a telephone call all the time she was here.'

'She didn't seem agitated or upset in any way?'

'Beryl was never agitated or upset. She was so lady-like, I simply can't believe —'

'Now on the day itself,' Lawson cut in, having had quite enough of Mrs Benson's pathetic expressions of belief in somebody who quite obviously had proved herself a clever and determined crook. 'Now on the day itself, Friday, she went out of the house before breakfast, didn't she?'

'There wasn't anything unusual about that. She nearly always went out before breakfast, to get a breath of air and to see if the pony was all right.'

'Yes, but on this particular Friday she went into the garage and immobilised your husband's car.'

'I suppose she must have done.'

'One of your girls, Penny wasn't it, actually saw her coming out of the garage?'

'Yes. From the bedroom window. But she didn't think anything of it. Why should she? At the far end of the garage there are buckets and things they use for the pony.'

The inspector nodded. 'And when her so-called brother conveniently turned up —'

'You don't think he was her brother?' Muriel Benson asked sadly.

'Could have been, I suppose. But lover most likely, I'd say, rather than brother. You didn't actually see him did you? Or his car?'

'I didn't; no. Penny got a glimpse of the car from up-stairs.'

'A smart kid of yours, that one. And she thought it was a Volvo.'

'That's what she says. I'm afraid all cars are the same to me. Has that helped at all?'

'Not a lot,' the inspector was forced to admit. 'We've checked and made inquiries – are still doing so in fact – but there are a lot of Volvos up and down the country.'

Comparable checkings and inquiries had been made about the scarves with which the bank manager had been bound and gagged but as Lawson's henchman had reported to him, 'There are thousands of these things sold every week, every day probably, at Marks & Sparks and similar big stores in all the towns of England . . .'

'Of course Beryl Carpenter wouldn't be her real name,' the inspector continued with Mrs Benson. 'I suppose you never by any chance got a hint of any other name she might have?'

Muriel Benson put a hand quickly up to her mouth in that curious involuntary gesture which people use when something has come suddenly and unexpectedly to mind.

'Good gracious me,' she exclaimed. 'You've made me think of something. I *do* remember something now. About her name. It was the day of the fête and gymkhana. At the Rectory Field. When it was all over and we were just start-ing out for home some people went by in a car and a young man it called out, "Hallo Barbara, fancy seeing you here." Something like that. I'm not sure of the exact words but he did say "Barbara" I'm sure of that.

'I asked Beryl about it and she said that it was her second name, she was christened Beryl Barbara and Freddie always called her Barbara.'

'Freddie?'

'That was the young man's name apparently.'

'Did you get a look at him?'

'I saw him, yes. Just as the car went by.'

'Could you describe him, Mrs Benson?' It wasn't a very hopeful question.

'Describe him? Oh dear! Well, he was young, and I think he was dark. He was certainly good-looking. They looked like a jolly young party out for the day.'

'How many of them were there?'

'I think there were four. Yes, I'm sure there were. Two girls and two young men.'

'Would you know any of them again?'

Mrs Benson considered for a moment, then shook her head. 'I don't think so. I'm afraid not.'

'And the car?'

'It was certainly an open car. I suppose it was what they call a sports car.'

'What make?'

She shook her head again.

'Colour?'

'Was it red?'

'It might have been red. I'm not much good at cars, I'm afraid.'

Back in Amminster once more the inspector talked it over with his sergeant.

'It isn't much, admittedly, but it's the only new thing that has emerged, this young chap called Freddie in the sports car at the gymkhana who obviously knew the girl and called her "Barbara". Who runs the gymkhana?'

'Captain Jimmy Praed, the Hunt secretary.'

'Do you suppose there's any sort of record of what cars went to the thing?'

'The cars would have to pay for a place at the ringside no doubt, but I don't imagine there would be any record kept.'

'Nor do I.'

'I'll make inquiries, though. An open sports car, possibly red; four people in it. It's just possible somebody will know something about it. But people come to the Amminster gymkhana from all over the place these days and I wouldn't be optimistic.'

'Neither would I,' Inspector Lawson agreed gloomily, little knowing that something would soon be happening in Church Lane, Amminster, not a quarter of a mile away from the police station where he sat, which was going to give him the unexpected, vital break that he wanted.

X

Days merged into weeks, and imperceptibly the weeks grew into a month, into two months, since the Friday of the Amminster bank robbery.

The affair had long since ceased to have any attraction for the press; Amminster had had its brief moment of notoriety and as far as the daily papers were concerned the whole thing was the deadest of dead ducks.

Even so Vyvyan still opened his *Telegraph* each morning with a slight feeling of apprehension that the word would stare out at him, heading some paragraph of unwelcome import.

Barbara, breakfasting as she always did opposite him in pyjamas and dressing-gown, would watch him across the table.

Ever since they had started to live together she had been quick to attune herself to his thoughts; and, since the Amminster affair she seemed to have developed an uncanny flair for knowing exactly what was going through his mind.

The fact that he was still even faintly apprehensive made her ribaldly scornful.

'No luck? Not even a tiny paragraph about us? Not even a mention?'

It didn't amuse Vyvyan to be jeered at by a girl, but he was forced to realise that since Amminster something had happened to Barbara. She had always been mettlesome and tricky to handle, that was largely why she had appealed to him originally, now some sort of edge had been put on her; she had become the dominant and commanding figure in the partnership. He had no desire to talk about Amminster, but she was constantly harking back to it.

'When I was pressing that gun against the silly little man's shoulder – God, I felt good. It was like being in bed with you.'

'Thank goodness the police haven't found the thing,' Vyvyan answered. 'I don't understand why they haven't; but there it is, they haven't. Yet.'

'They won't.'

'I wish I were as sure about it as you are.'

'I can't think what's happened to you, Vyvyan; you've lost your nerve.'

Vyvyan flushed; he didn't relish hearing a woman say that to him.

'And I can't imagine why,' Barbara hammered on at him. 'It was you who had the idea in the first place. The perfect crime. You came home that night and told me you had talked about it with that legal man and his boy-friend. And then you went down to stay with those people near Amminster and worked the whole thing out. You must admit that.'

'I've never said otherwise. But it wasn't the perfect crime. We did what everybody seems to do. Get in too much of a hurry once the action started and made a most colossal boob.'

'Which hasn't been discovered.'

'We still made it.'

'For God's sake, man, it doesn't matter making a boob if nobody finds us out. What we wanted is money. And we've got it. Twenty-seven thousand pounds of it. I enjoyed getting it; and, by God, am I going to enjoy spending it!'

One evening Barbara switched on the TV at random and they found themselves looking at a documentary about life in Wandsworth prison. Barbara was for switching off again, or changing the channel, but Vyvyan motioned her to let it go on.

He seemed morbidly fascinated by the programme and

96

when it ended said, 'That's what I'm afraid of – being shut up.'

Barbara laughed scornfully and mixed herself a drink.

'Nobody's going to shut me up. I can tell you that,' she said.

Her inclination was to start using the stolen money right away, and she could only just be persuaded to agree with Vyvyan's more cautious advice in the matter.

She probably would not have agreed with it except that directly after Amminster financial affairs became easier for them.

Having left T.M. & F. at the shortest of short notices, hardly sure himself whether he had flounced out or been kicked out, Vyvyan was lucky enough to get a better job with a rival firm almost immediately.

He was warned from the start that it was only a temporary post – outside help was needed to cope with one particular, and particularly valuable, assignment – and he understood that when the *ad hoc* job was finished he would be unemployed again.

But while it lasted he was well paid; and he certainly needed to be because Barbara was intent on helping him to spend every pound he made.

Now it was the Lobster Pot almost every night, and although it was out of character for Vyvyan to sound a note of caution where spending money was concerned he did once feel constrained to say, 'Don't forget I shall have to pay income tax on what I'm being paid for this job.'

'For God's sake,' Barbara flared back at him. 'Everybody has to pay income tax. What's the good of worrying about it? And it won't happen till next year and by then we'll be using the twenty-seven thousand quid.'

Vyvyan looked anxiously to left and right. Luckily there was nobody immediately near them, but all the same he said angrily, 'I wonder you don't stand up on the table and tell everybody at the top of your voice exactly what happened.'

'I've a damned good mind to,' Barbara laughed, 'And if I did I don't suppose anyone would believe me. If you keep your head and put a bold face on it you can get away with murder.'

Barbara missed her job at the Two Vs, it simply wasn't in her nature to sit mooning in the flat all day waiting to amuse the lord and master of the household when he came back from work.

Certainly she was ready enough to amuse him; Vyvyan was even a little alarmed sometimes by her insatiate eagerness for the sport of the bedroom; but she wanted something to occupy her during the day.

'Work out another job somewhere and I'll go as an au pair again,' she urged only half in jest.

'For Pete's sake, woman, you must be stark, staring mad. This business at Amminster has gone to your head. The whole essence of the thing as far as we are concerned is *once and once only*. In and out. That's where the police get baffled. We've never done a job before so they've nothing to refer back to, no *modus operandi* or anything like that to latch on to. No fingerprints, no photographs. Nothing. And you can take it from me that we are never going to do anything else. We've thrown our line in and caught our fish and that's the end of it for me. No more fishing. I'm satisfied with what I've got.'

'Men are so damned unadventurous. They're always satisfied with what they've got. Women aren't; ever.'

Salvation loomed up for her in the shape of Stella Margerrison whom she met at a charity affair at Park Lane in which the worlds of the theatre and the antique business were liberally mixed; one seeking publicity, the other trade. 'Advertisement and old fakes' as one sardonic columnist put it.

Lady Margerrison was deceptively *petite* and fragile in appearance. Standing next to her at a drinks party, dry Martini or Champagne cocktail in hand, you began to wonder if she ever talked sense; if you came up against her in business you very soon discovered that in those circumstances she very seldom talked anything else. And hard, practical, cash-conscious common sense at that.

She had a real talent for interior decorating and with some initial success behind her now wanted to launch out into something bigger.

What she was looking for was a partner.

And the partner she was looking for had to have two qualifications: a sympathy with, and some knowledge of, good furniture and fittings; and cash.

Stella Margerrison was hoping to find these things in a woman. There had already been a number of men in her life and, with her looks and figure there could always be plenty more – had she so desired.

She and Barbara took to one another from the first moment of casual introduction; and, always a person to be guided by instinct, Stella brusquely dismissed the man she had been talking to and concentrated on Barbara.

'I could get plenty of men to come in as partner,' she was soon explaining; 'but I don't want a man. I want a woman. Don't be nervous, I'm not a lesbian. Nothing like that. But just for the moment anyway, I've had men. Too complicated and messy. Especially in business. And there really is a business to be built up here. I've got some very useful connections and I've got some good friends on the glossies, so we could be sure of getting a useful paragraph every now and again. "*I hear that the new luxury penthouse decorated by Lady Margerison for the Persian oil magnate is quite fabulously beautiful,*" you know the sort of thing.

'I've seen the ideal place in Curzon Terrace, but I can't get started there without money. I daresay I could borrow from the bank; but they want eight per cent or whatever it is interest and that's going to knock the profits about. I've not the slightest doubt that if partnership in the business included a season ticket into bed with me that I could get some men to put up the money. But I don't want it that way; I've explained about that —'

'How much money do you want?' Barbara asked.

'I think you and I could get on famously together,' Stella said.

'So do I.'

'You could hold the fort at the shop while I'm out interviewing clients.'

'That's more or less what I used to do at Tooveys. How much money would you want me to put in?'

'I don't suppose we should make a penny for the first year; the second year we ought to break even; and after that with any luck we ought to begin to coin the stuff, so anything you put in is in the nature of an investment really.'

'Suits me,' Barbara laughed. 'I'm looking for something to invest in. How much?'

This conversation she reported to Vyvyan when she got back to Hambledon Street.

'And how much does she want?' he asked.

'I've agreed to put up five thousand pounds.'

'And if you suddenly weigh in with five thousand pounds in notes won't it look a little odd? Don't you think someone may start wondering where it all came from?'

'Yes, I think they might. But I've allowed for that.'

'You've allowed for it? How?'

'I've offered to pay Stella fifty pounds a week as a contribution to rent and rates. My articled pupil's fee if you like to call it that. That's to go on for the first two years. I get a salary during that time and at the end of two years I start getting a cut of the profits. Sixty-forty in her favour for one year, fifty-fifty after that.

'Fifty pound notes mixed in each week with the rest of the cash won't cause suspicion anywhere.'

'Doesn't Stella Margerrison think it a bit strange your wanting to pay the money that way?'

'I don't know what she thinks. I didn't ask her. I said

that's how I was willing to do it and she said O.K., it suited her that way. She agreed.'

Vyvyan hadn't wanted to start using the money out of the suitcases for six months, but already more than two months had gone by without any suggestion of danger, and in any case it was clear that Barbara had made up her mind.

She said so; now.

She said, 'You may as well accept the fact, Vyvyan, that that's what I intend to do. So let's have a drink on it, eh?'

Vyvyan mixed the drinks without speaking.

Going into partnership with Stella Margerrison proved to be exactly the sort of job Barbara had been looking for. All sorts of frustrating difficulties had to be overcome; there were delays and misunderstandings with lawyers, there were broken promises and lagging schedules from the builders; but there was never any difference or dispute between the two women themselves.

Each liked and admired the other.

'What I like about you, Bar, is your go-getting approach. What you want you go after and get,' Stella said one day.

Barbara laughed; for an instant she was faintly tempted to boast of just how successful her go-getting approach had been; but she contented herself by saying, 'It's astonishing what you can get if you go about it the right way and take enough trouble over it.'

Every week she handed fifty pounds in notes to her partner who did not seem in any way surprised at being paid in notes instead of by cheque and never raised the slightest query about it.

Relations between the two women were not in any way impaired when Barbara began an affair with a man who, as an old friend and supporter of Stella's, came several times to Curzon Terrace to see how things were progressing there.

This man, a member of the House of Lords, was married and had a wife and family firmly established in a frequently photographed country house in the Home Counties. At home he did all the proper things and did them well – the large subscription to the local Hunt, the chairmanship of the Conservative Association, the presidency of the cricket club, the vice-chairmanship of the Hospital Board, the governorship of the Girls' Public School: all these duties were conscientiously performed.

Off the leash in his flat in Half Moon Street he considered he had earned the right to take a somewhat broader view of life.

Whether he had ever been Stella Margerrison's lover Barbara didn't know and didn't care.

The man came into her life at a time when she was hungry for fresh excitement and he supplied it. Since this second affair was conducted entirely in the afternoons it didn't impinge on what Barbara had by now come to regard as her home life in Hambledon Street and, exercising the self-delusion which people find it so easy to use in such circumstances, she told herself that she did not see any reason why it should affect her relationship with Vyvyan Weighman.

Yet – unspoken, unconfessed, unacknowledged, unreferred to – it did somehow affect them.

Barbara was still willing, even anxious, to meet any demands made by Vyvyan in bed. She flattered herself that she was just as good as ever. Yet, even in the moments of wild satisfaction Vyvyan was aware somehow that it was not quite as it had been.

An even more frenzied approach didn't make things any better.

There was a difference and he was conscious of it.

Since Amminster everything, including Barbara, had changed; and, in spite of the money stacked away and of the fact that theoretically money was what he wanted most in the world, Vyvyan began to be sorry that he had ever indulged in that discussion about 'the perfect crime'.

102

Nowadays he was drinking considerably more. Mrs Bennett, in The Brave Bombardier, noticed it, but naturally made no comment.

Although he had left T.M. & F. Vyvyan still used the Bombardier; it was reasonably close to his new offices and Mrs Bennett was there.

Although nothing beyond the civilities of greetings and platitudes about the weather had ever passed between them Vyvyan was fascinated by the woman.

He would stand in his accustomed place at the bar, his drink in front of him, watching her move expertly about her business, trying (and failing) to analyse the magnetism that she possessed.

And thinking that if ever he could summon up the courage to ask her 'What's gone wrong?' (which he knew he never would do) she might be able to tell him.

One morning in the Bombardier there happened one of those coincidences by which life so often confounds art.

It was after half past two. Vyvyan should have been back at work but was still standing there, the latest in an overlong series of drinks in front of him. He was watching Mrs Bennett and the customary thoughts and speculations about her were running in his head.

It was at that precise moment that the other figure at the bar, who might have carried round his neck a placard 'The Last of the Bohemians' so exactly in dress appearance and manner did he look the part, it was at that precise moment that this character leant over the bar and daring to wag what seemed to be almost an admonitory forefinger at Mrs Bennett demanded, 'What's gone wrong with it all? Tell me that. What's gone wrong?'

The words so precisely matched the thoughts running through Vyvyan's head that he was startled.

The Last Bohemian, who after ten o'clock any morning was seldom exactly sober and equally seldom really drunk, leant even farther across the bar in an access of alcoholic philosophy.

'I'll tell you what's gone wrong, Ethel,' he said. (*'Ethel'!* Vyvyan was equally astonished at the man's impudence and intrigued by the name). 'I'll tell you what's gone wrong.

'God should never have split the first human being up into man and woman. That's where the mistake was. Way back in the Garden of Eden. That first human being was O.K. Why wouldn't he be, made in the image of God? Man and woman mixed. The original unisex. That's what he was. The perfect combination.

'Then God got spiteful and wanted to take it out on us for some reason or other so he got a chopper and cut us down the middle. Made two of us. Like cutting a worm in two halves with a spade just to watch it squirm. Male and female he created them. And ever since then we've been in trouble. You're not complete in yourself; nobody is; so everyone's for ever going round looking for the other half to join up with. And of course you don't find it. The human bloody predicament. That's what's gone wrong. There was Paradise once and we've lost it. That's what's bloody well gone wrong.'

'There's no need to use bad language even if you do feel that way about it,' Mrs Bennett said reprovingly.

The Last of the Bohemians flicked a forefinger towards the broad brim of his floppy hat; looked at her for a long two seconds; smiled; uttered the single word *'Ethel'*; and went out.

It was very seldom that Mrs Bennett spoke about one customer to another. But now she did. The silence that followed the Bohemian's theatrical exit was eventually broken by her comment on the situation.

Busily polishing a glass (she was almost fanatical in her care of the Bombardier glasses) she said – to herself? to the shining glass? perhaps even to Vyvyan? – 'There was Paradise once and we've lost it. What a thing to say!'

'I don't know that I believe much in Paradise,' Vyvyan

answered. 'Paradise is for parsons. As far as I'm concerned you want something, you go after it, and somehow it slips away.'

Mrs Bennett replaced the now brilliantly clear glass on a shelf and selected another for treatment.

'Is that what has happened to you?' she asked.

It was a moment before Vyvyan answered; a moment in which all the self-pitying, self-flagelleting, sweetly-sharp comforts of the confessional rose in his mind to tempt him.

There was nobody else in the bar; he was convinced that if he told everything to Mrs Bennett she would be neither shocked nor surprised, and that the mere act of telling, of pronouncing the truth aloud for another human being's ears to hear, would be an immense relief.

But, of course, he didn't do it.

People seldom act as far out of character as that.

All he allowed himself to say was, 'If it has, it's my own fault.'

He would have liked to add the word 'Ethel' just for devilment, but his courage failed him.

He added nothing; he finished his drink and went out into the afternoon sunshine of London.

Mrs Bennett continued to polish her glasses.

To Vyvyan's annoyance the well-paid, temporary job he was doing necessitated a trip to Dewsbury to verify some facts on the spot.

Barbara, hearing the news, affected the conventional *de rigueur* amusement.

She and Vyvyan were equally parochial. Anything north of Islington was Esquimaux land as far as they were concerned.

'Dewsbury? Where on earth is that?'

'Yorkshire – the heavy woollen part apparently.'

'Remember to take your heavy woollies with you, it will be cold up in them thar hills. And a flat cloth cap. It will endear you to the natives. Will you be staying the night?'

'I'm afraid so. Two nights in fact. I've got two factories to visit and it means a day at each. I don't suppose there's much point in my saying behave yourself while I'm away; but since we seem to be on rather more formal terms than we used to be I'll make the request all the same.'

Barbara laughed.

In her early days with Vyvyan she had been careful to mind her Ps and Qs; just once or twice she had been slightly scared of his dark and unpredictable moods. But that feeling of caution had long since worn off. Particularly since Amminster. Since Amminster she had been in the ascendant. She had become the predominant partner and she knew it.

She was engaged in a successful business venture; she had a lover; she still enjoyed living in Hambledon Street.

She knew that Vyvyan knew that she had a lover; but she also knew that circumstances forced him to pretend not to know.

The situation stimulated and amused her.

So now she laughed gaily and said, 'Have you ever had the slightest reason for supposing that I would not, as you rather quaintly put it, behave myself?'

'There are lots of things I don't feel sure about these days.'

'You're weakening,' Barbara told him. 'There's nothing I don't feel sure about. Mix two more drinks.'

Vyvyan went up to Yorkshire on Tuesday morning, and in the evening of that day, shortly after seven, Barbara sat on the long low stool in front of the electric fire in the living-room of Hambledon Street. She was glowing with warmth after a delicious long, pine-y bath and she was wearing a new gold dress that she knew instinctively to be just right for her.

She sat in front of the fire finishing the painting of her nails.

She didn't bother to look at the ormulu clock because she knew she had plenty of time. Her lover from Half Moon Street was taking her out to dine and dance at the Palamino but he was not due to call for her until a quarter to eight.

When the bell sounded she did look at the time; she was surprised; the clock showed hardly twenty past seven.

She thought it unlikely that her escort would be twenty-five minutes early; yet who else, at that hour, would it be?

With the fingers of her left hand outstretched (the nails were still drying) she went to the front door of the flat and opened it.

The man standing there smiled at her.

'Good evening,' he said in his smooth, soft voice.

She was astonished to see him.

XI

Detective Inspector Lawson re-read the report he had been studying and then put it away in the folder with the rest.

He pushed the bulging folder away from him across the desk with a slight gesture of annoyance.

No good letting yourself get irritated; he knew that; yet if you cared about your job in the way he did it undeniably *was* irritating to see a case slipping away from you.

Recently one or two letters had appeared in the *Advertiser* couched in the usual sarcastic language of your clever local know-all suggesting that instead of harrying motorists for minor, and sometimes only technical, offences the police would do better to concentrate on real crime and criminals. 'When are we going to hear any news about the thieves who carried out a daring raid on Barrolds bank in High Parade?' the writer of one letter demanded, 'Or have the police conveniently forgotten about them?'

Inspector Lawson had certainly not forgotten about the raid on Barrolds bank. Despite the pressure of other work there was hardly a day when he didn't think about it.

One of the platitudes which he was fond of repeating to his sergeant was, 'Something always turns up. If you look at a thing long enough, worry away at it, something always turns up.'

He had great hopes that this had happened in the Barrolds bank case when Muriel Benson suddenly remembered about the young man in the red sports car at the gymkhana who called out 'Barbara'.

It wasn't possible to identify every car that had been at the gymkhana, but by patient questioning Lawson reckoned that he, or his sergeant, had been able to trace well over half of them.

Two of the owners they spoke to thought they remembered the car in question. In fact one of them was sure that he had seen it. He remembered a party of four young people sitting down to a picnic meal behind the car. 'They had a little table, one of those folding affairs, and chairs. And plenty of bottles about. Doing things in style. Enjoying themselves.'

'And the make of the car? Its registration number? What the four people really looked like?'

The inspector's informant shook his head to all these things. 'I had my kids there, watching the jumping. I just remember seeing this other lot eating at the back of their car, but I didn't take any particular notice. Why should I? I wasn't all that interested, was I?'

So what for a time had looked like being the 'something which always turns up' petered away into nothing; and now the inspector having almost automatically looked through the bulky Barrolds bank file yet another fruitless time pushed it away from him.

There was a rap at the door and the desk sergeant put his head inside the room – a habit which annoyed the inspector; he liked people to be either in or out of his office; not halfway.

'Come in,' he said irritably, 'come in.'

'It's Todd, sir. He'd like a word with you.'

'Todd? It's not his day.'

'That's right, sir. But this isn't about the garden apparently.'

Inspector Lawson was a keen gardener, and had long since taken over charge of the sizeable bit of ground in front of the station. Occasionally he did some work in it himself, but it was mainly cared for by a jobbing gardener, Frederick Charles Todd of 52 Church Lane, who came one half day a week to cut the grass, trim the edges and generally keep the place tidy.

109

'You'd better tell him to come in, then,' Lawson said.

Frederick Charles Todd came in. He was a man of fifty or thereabouts. Physically on the small side; mentally of very strong convictions, being an Elder in the Church of the People of The Fellowship, a fundamentalist sect who had a thriving centre in Amminster.

Privately the inspector thought all religious sects were slightly bonkers; but he knew Todd to be a decent little man and he respected him.

'Well, Todd,' he greeted him, 'what can I do for you?'

In reply the gardener laid on the Inspector's table a pistol.

'What's this, then?' Lawson asked, surprised.

'I'm sorry to tell you I found that in my garden, Mr Lawson.'

'In your garden, in Church Lane?'

'I'm not going to try to hide anything, one of my lads had it.'

'You'd better tell me about it then, hadn't you?'

'That's what I've come here for, Mr Lawson. You've seen my two lads, of course. Terry, the oldest, he's ten. And I've got my worries with him, I can tell you that. There's a gang of older boys at the school and he's managed to get in with them. A proper lot of young devils some of them, but Terry thinks they're wonderful.

'The wife said, well, if you're going to tell them they mustn't knock about in the streets you've got to give them something to do at home. Which I saw the sense of. So I gave them a hand building this house in a tree.

'It was Terry's idea in the first place; there was an article in one of the papers he gets every week. How to build a house in a tree. A do-it-yourself idea. I don't know if you remember, but at the back of those Church Lane cottages the gardens run down to the old brook and along the edge of it there are two or three decent-sized trees.

'I've always got a few odd bits of timber in the shed so

one way and another we were able to make quite a good little hut place – a platform with sides to it, it was really – in this beech tree.

'I got quite keen about it and the wife said I enjoyed doing it more than the boys did. She was about right, too; but once it was made I left them to play games in it.

'I don't say it kept them off the streets altogether, they still go out bird's-nesting occasionally and that sort of thing, but it certainly helped.'

Lawson nodded. 'I wish other fathers did the same,' he said. 'And the gun?'

'I'm coming to that. That was yesterday. I was doing a spot of painting in the shed and I wanted a touch of aluminium. I knew I had a small pot of aluminium paint somewhere, but could I find it?

'I looked everywhere and in the end I thought I wonder if those young devils have taken it up in the tree for any reason.

'I thought I'd get up into that house of theirs and see just what they had collected up there.

'So I climbed up this ladder-staircase business to have a look.

'Never mind about any aluminium paint. I forgot all about that. The first thing I saw was this gun.

'I don't mind telling you it startled me.

'If there's one thing I hate it's firearms and shooting, all this violence stuff you see on TV and read in the papers.

'The two boys were out at the time, but as soon as they were back I got on to them about it pretty sharpish, I can tell you.'

'And what had they got to say about it?' Lawson asked.

'Terry had had it up there for weeks apparently. He and his brother were out bird's-nesting one morning and Terry found this gun lying in the grass pretty well at the side of the road. He just picked it up.'

'At the side of which road?'

'Swilley Lane.'

William Lawson remained outwardly impassive, but inwardly he felt a little thrill of excitement.

'Swilley Lane was where Mr Benson of the bank was tied up and gagged,' he said.

'I know it was. That's what I thought of at once. My God, I thought, I don't want my lads mixed up in anything like that. I've always been respectable, you know that, Mr Lawson.'

'Don't worry, Todd. Your boys weren't mixed up in the bank business, and nobody's going to suggest they were.'

'No; but I thought the best thing I could do was to bring the gun down here and tell you all about it.'

'Very sensible of you. Now, is it possible to fix the exact day and the time when your lad found this thing? . . .'

Before long the detective inspector, now with all his keenness for the scent alive again, was recounting the substance of the Todd interview to his sergeant.

'What have I always told you? Look at a thing long enough; stare at it; worry at it and something turns up.'

The sergeant considered that what had turned up was a colossal stroke of luck. But he didn't think it diplomatic to say so, and in any case luck was a necessary part of the job; if the breaks didn't go your way occasionally you weren't likely to get anywhere.

'What's more we've got the date and the time fixed,' Lawson went on. 'The two lads had to be at the Filston Road baths by eleven because it was the day of the inter-school swimming sports, so Terry is sure they must have been bird's-nesting along Swilley Lane just about half past nine.'

'Which makes sense, it fits in.'

'I reckon the timetable must have gone something like this: the two villains bundled Benson, tied and gagged, out of the car as near nine as makes no matter. In bundling him out the gun was accidentally pushed out with him.

'In the hurry and flurry neither of them noticed it; very likely each thought the other was looking after it.

'It's the sort of mistake every villain is likely to make, thank goodness, else I don't know what our crime detective figures would look like. They spend weeks talking the thing over to make sure that they won't make a boob, but when it comes to the crunch everything is quicker and more exciting than they allowed for and one of them forgets, or overlooks, something.

'After a while, as we know, Benson got over the worst of his fright and began to try to do something for himself.

'He kicked about and struggled a good deal with the result that he dislodged himself from the sort of shelf where they had put him and rolled down the grass bank to the farm track at the bottom.

'While he was crawling along the farm track and being picked up by farmer Lacey and so on, Todd's boys came along Swilley Lane on their bird's-nesting expedition and found the gun.'

'And that young Terry just took it home and kept it hidden all this time?'

Lawson laughed. 'Can you blame him? Damn it, he's only a kid. He's a lively lad. He thought it was a real gun, of course, and what boy isn't going to be excited at finding that lying about? Then he knew how his father felt about guns and violence and that he wouldn't be allowed to keep the thing so naturally enough he took it to his special hideyhole up in the tree and it became a dead secret between the two boys.

'But when the news about the bank robbery came out in the local paper that evening —'

'When that happened of course the boys must have realised that the gun in Swilley Lane very probably had something to do with it and you can bet your boots they were scared.

'The gun was safely hidden up the tree; nobody but

themselves knew anything about it; they decided to keep it that way. There's nothing any normal kid enjoys more than a secret, something hidden from the grown-ups.'

The sergeant nodded. He thought the inspector had given a very likely account of what had happened. He turned his attention to the gun.

'I suppose Todd thought it was a real one?' he said.

'Lord, yes. It might have been a stick of sweating gelignite from the way he handled it. He was obviously afraid it might go off at any moment.'

'It's the kind of thing you see used in amateur theatricals,' the sergeant said, he having done a good bit in that line in his day.

Lawson wasn't interested in amateur theatricals.

'The question is can we find out something about it. Where it came from. Who sold it and who bought it and so on,' he insisted.

Both men once more examined the dummy weapon thoroughly.

It was made of metal, but was a good deal lighter than steel and it reproduced faithfully all the features of a real gun.

Seeing that it had been handled daily by two boys over a period of some ten weeks and had obviously been polished into the bargain Lawson had already discounted any likelihood of getting anything useful in the way of fingerprints off it.

The only obvious mark was on the base of the butt where a capital K was embossed within a circle.

The inspector knew singularly little about firearms, but was human enough not to want to say so in front of a junior.

'I suppose there's somebody at forensic who might know all about these things,' the sergeant suggested.

'Could be. They're quite sure they know everything there. As it happens I've got to go there tomorrow so I'll

114

take it with me.'

At 'forensic' in County headquarters the inspector was made to feel rather foolish.

'If we want to know anything about firearms,' a bright young know-all told him, 'we get on to Amminster.'

'Amminster?'

'The university. Professor Caplan.'

The inspector knew a great deal about the town of Amminster and many of the people in it. But he didn't know them all. He didn't know Professor Caplan. In fact he had never heard of him.

'He's an expert, then, is he?' he asked cautiously.

'*The* expert. He's made a hobby of it. Like some people collect stamps or old silver or what-have-you Professor Caplan collects firearms. He knows it all.'

Back home that evening Lawson sought, and received, further information from his daughter Lucy, reading a course of sociology at the University of Amminster.

Lucy was an uninhibited, free-thinking, tradition-mocking nineteen.

'Professor Caplan?' she queried. 'You mean Tarzan?'

'Is that what you call him?'

'Tarzan or the Naked Ape. I wonder your minions haven't had him up for indecent exposure half a dozen times already.'

'Is that the sort of thing he does?' Lawson asked, feeling a little flummoxed.

'Notorious for it. I don't say he was absolutely the first man to use a zip instead of fly-buttons but I'm sure he approved of the invention.'

William Lawson was old-fashioned enough to feel rather shocked.

At eleven o'clock next morning he was sitting in the professor's room at the university trying to keep his mind on the subject of his visit and not on the incidental information Lucy had so cheerfully supplied.

Lawson had a vaguely reverential notion about university professors so that Caplan, on the young side of forty with a woolly head of hair and an unkempt beard and wearing a dirty yellow pullover and jeans, hardly came up to expectations as far as appearances went.

But it wasn't about sartorial matters that Lawson had come to see him. It was about firearms; and on that subject the professor came up to expectations handsomely.

He picked up the gun which Lawson put before him and studied it with tolerant amusement.

'Of course I don't have to tell you it's a fake, it's not real.'

Lawson nodded. 'Yes. I know that much about it,' he said.

'It's an exact replica, mind you. But of course if you put a bullet in it and fired it the whole thing would blow up in your face. It's the sort of thing they use on the stage and in pageants.'

'Is there any chance of knowing where it came from?'

'Oh Lord, yes. Every chance. If you remember I devoted a whole chapter in my book on modern firearms to these fakes, dummies, whatever you like to call them.'

As the inspector hadn't even heard of *Modern Firearms*, illustrated by photographs and published by the Modern World Press at the intimidating price of fifteen pounds, he wisely kept quiet.

Professor Caplan indicated the K on the base of the butt.

'That tells us where it comes from,' he said, 'even if we hadn't guessed already. K stands for *Koyato* a Japanese firm who make Christmas crackers and toys, theatrical props and things like that. Their stuff is flooding the English market at the moment.'

He broke open the gun and smiled with satisfaction when he found what he was looking for.

'I expect you noticed this,' he said, indicating 2.73 stamped in very small figures on the inside of one of the six chambers.

Lawson, who in fact had not noticed the tiny figures, and who was ashamed of the fact, wasn't going to say so.

'I suppose it's to do with the calibre?' he hazarded.

Caplan laughed rather rudely. 'Good Lord, no. Who cares about the calibre of these dummy things, anyway? It's Koyato's check on the shipment date. 2.73. February nineteen seventy-three.'

'You mean to say that this particular gun was shipped to England in February of this year?'

'It must have been.'

'And this Koyato firm – they've got a branch or something over here?'

'They must have a representative of some sort,' the professor said. 'I should have thought the police could find that out easily enough.'

'Don't worry, Professor,' Lawson promised. 'We'll find that out all right.'

'I'm glad to have your assurance,' Caplan said. 'Sometimes I wonder what the police do besides interfering with perfectly harmless demonstrations.'

'*Catch naked apes*,' the inspector felt like saying; but he held his peace. Even if he didn't like the woolly-haired professor he felt grateful to him.

Lawson came away from the university in a jubilant frame of mind. No one knew better than himself that if any investigation was going to get anywhere it needed an encouraging smile from Lady Luck.

The inspector realised that he had just had his nod from the lady, and he meant to lose no time at all in co-operating with it.

By four o'clock the following afternoon he was sitting in an expensively furnished office in Regent Street being told by an almost aggressively sexy secretary that Mr Gaythorne was taking a trunk call but wouldn't keep him more than a minute or two.

117

Even William Lawson, who liked to think that age and experience had case-hardened him, could feel the waves of femininity emanating from the curvaceous creature. Good job old Professor Tarzan isn't here, he thought, we should probably have a scene . . .

Mr Gaythorne, when the trunk call was finished and he became available, proved to be young, enthusiastic and very obviously in the money.

He was negotiating the sale of so many Koyato goods every month that he could hardly bank his commissions fast enough.

He was organised, too.

Once the problem was put to him it didn't take him long, with the sex bomb's help, to turn up the relevant leters and documents.

'That lot in February went to Davis & Foster,' he said.

'Davis & Foster?'

'Toy & games wholesalers. In the city. Look up their exact address, Valerie.'

After a moment's absence Valerie came back into the room carrying a volume of the London telephone directory which – Lawson noted with fascination – only just escaped total submersion in her voluminous front.

'Sixteen Poulter's Place,' she announced.

'And they will have handled this individual gun?' Lawson asked.

'Undoubtedly,' Gaythorne assured him. 'The February shipment was all toys and games and that sort of thing and it went to them.'

Lawson thanked him and went out to hail a taxi.

It didn't surprise him in the least that one was cruising past as he stepped out on to the pavement.

He had experienced this sort of thing before – for weeks a frustrating negative whichever way you turned, then all of a sudden, like the first log shifting in a river-jam, something gives way and a whole lot of things follow; you find yourself in the hunt again.

That a taxi should be ready to hand was only one more sign that luck was going his way for a change.

Poulter's Place was narrow and dark, and the doorways of its tall uninviting buildings bore brass plates with all sorts of strange names on them.

Among the Fenskis and the Leopold Stowskis, the D'Avidgolds and the Guildermeyers the homely Davis & Foster stood out like Doctor Livingstone in Africa.

Inside Davis & Foster's the alert young man said, 'Well, I can't absolutely swear of course that we sold this individual gun but it's ninety-nine per cent certain that we must have done. It's a Koyato job and it's got their date stamp for February this year so I reckon you can take it that it was part of the consignment we had from them in that month.'

'A big consignment?'

'The whole consignment, yes; very big. The point about these foreign firms is; you order the goods, you get the goods. On time. You order goods in this country and when everybody is back from their long week-end the shop stewards get together to decide whether the Union rules will permit any work to be done or not. Then if the things get made the transport people or the railways have most likely got a "go-slow" on; by the time you ultimately get the stuff the foreigner has scooped the market.

'We got a lot of stuff in February, but it was nearly all what we class "large juveniles" – toy tricycles, toy wheel-barrows, things of that sort. As far as I remember we didn't have more than a couple of dozen of these things. I can check it, of course.'

'And you can check whom you sold them to?'

The young man grinned amiably, 'A bit of a bind,' he said, 'but could do. Yes.'

'Whom do you sell to?'

'Nearly all our stuff is sold by post. We send a catalogue out each year to over six thousand addresses. Costs a fortune at today's prices, I can tell you. We have got a rep who works the London district; but it's largely postal.'

'Shops or individuals?'

'Well, both. But shops mostly. Toy shops; general stores with a toy counter; a certain number of curio and antique dealers. If you wait a bit I'll see what I can find out.'

'I'll wait,' the inspector assured him. 'I'm good at waiting. We have to be.'

He didn't have to wait unduly long.

'Here we are, then,' the young man said, spreading a mass of flimsy typewritten sheets on the desk. 'I was right about the number. We only had two dozen of these guns. More to make up the order than anything else, they are a shade outside our normal line.'

'And do you know where you sold them to?'

'Yes. I've got it here. We got a postal order for a dozen from Jennings of Birmingham. We sell a lot of stuff to them. And our London rep got rid of the others, half a dozen to Mackworth in Praed Street and half a dozen to a shop called Tooveys, just off Sloane Square.'

Having made a note of all the relevant names and addresses the inspector thanked the young man heartily and made his way down the rickety stairs into Poulter's Place again.

The machinery would have to be set in motion to deal with Jennings of Birmingham, but the inspector did not think that much good would come out of that. He felt instinctively that the Amminster job had been London based and he decided to lose no time in following up the two London possibilities.

Mackworth's in Praed Street sold stationery, paperbacks, sweets, tobacco and toys.

The gentleman in charge, whose cast of countenance strongly suggested that Mackworth was not his family name, reacted vigorously when Lawson produced the dummy gun.

'My God,' he exclaimed. 'More trouble with them? What is it now? Who's put you on to me this time?'

Lawson suggested that he should calm down and take it easy; all that was happening was that a few simple inquiries were being made.

'I wish I'd never bought the things,' the man said. 'Davis & Foster's rep talked me into taking half a dozen – here, wait a minute —' He dodged into the back premises and reappeared after a few seconds with a large cardboard box.

'There you are. Six of 'em. Half a dozen. Just as they were delivered to me. A dead loss.'

'So you haven't sold any?'

'I wasn't allowed to. I thought they'd sell like hot cakes to the lads round here, but I hadn't had one on show in the window for a day before the Militant Mums were round.'

'Militant Mums?'

'Well, that's what I call 'em. the women round here, church people mostly, have got together to try to stop all this violence the kids get up to in the streets. One of their big things is no toy firearms or things of that sort to be sold. It's all going to be loving-kindness and bless everybody apparently. So if I didn't take these guns out of my window and stop selling 'em my shop was going to be boycotted. Some loving-kindness I call that. Well, you can't fight the women. I learnt that a long time ago. You can do a lot of things beginning with f to 'em, but you can't fight 'em, mister. Not to make any sense.

'So there they are. All six of 'em. In the box. Unsold. And won't be sold now, either. A dead loss, like I said.'

The inspector expressed polite regret about Mackworth's trading difficulties, but secretly he was delighted.

Nothing could have suited him better; at a stroke twenty-five per cent of the leads he thought he would have to follow up had been eliminated. Indeed, fifty per cent of the London leads; and he now hastened off to deal with the others.

Tooveys, just off Sloane Square, was vastly different in character and general ambience from Mackworth's of Praed Street.

Lawson felt an odd little frisson of excitement as he ducked his head and made his way into the rather dark interior.

There was no other customer there, and a large corpulent man came out of the small office place in the rear.

Presumably the proprietor, Lawson thought; and from the first instant he knew that he didn't like the man.

He announced who he was and produced his warrant card to prove it.

He got the impression, strongly, that his instinctive feeling of dislike was not one-sided and that the large man with the flabby white face had no love for the police either.

I wonder if he's ever been in trouble, Lawson thought, and knew that the matter could, and would, be checked in a matter of hours.

'Mr Toovey?'

'Venning. There isn't any Toovey.'

'I wonder if you could help me, Mr Venning.'

Peter Venning didn't give any indication whether he was willing to help the police or not; he stood there studying the inspector with his rather large eyes in that pallid face.

Lawson produced a plastic bag and drew the dummy gun out of it.

Venning watched and said nothing.

'I understand that in February of this year you bought half a dozen of these guns from Davis & Foster of Poulter's Place?'

'What of it?'

'Have you sold them?'

'I sold one. I've still got five in stock.'

'You've sold one only? Whom did you sell it to, Mr Venning?'

Peter Venning had two strong characteristics: an irrational animosity against the police and anything to do with them; and a love of intrigue for its own sake.

His feeling against the police stemmed from an affair now some years old in which a close friend of his had been (as Venning described it) 'hounded' by the police because of suspected homosexual irregularities. Venning had never forgotten this, and ever since the affair his views about the police had lost all pretence to reason or logic.

'You're asking a lot of questions,' he now said. 'What's all this in aid of?'

'Do you know a place called Amminster?' Lawson asked.

Venning considered; shook his head; no, he didn't know Amminster; and watching him the inspector didn't think that he did.

'Why?'

'On April the twenty-third of this year the manager of Barrolds bank in Amminster was held up at gun-point and the bank was robbed. There are reasonable grounds for thinking that this was the gun that was used. It's not certain, but it's very likely.'

Venning remained silent again for some seconds; Lawson found these silences a little off-putting; he wondered what in hell the flabby pale-faced man was thinking about during them.

'And who used the gun?' Venning asked at length.

Lawson laughed. 'I wish I knew. It was a woman. Youngish, good-looking, well spoken. Fond of riding. She had got herself a job as an au pair in the bank manager's house and worked the job that way. I don't say the manager tried on anything with her. I don't think he did. But from all accounts she was very attractive and I think he lost his head a bit and probably let out a number of things to her he should have kept quiet about.'

'And you don't know her name?'

Once again Lawson said, 'Almost certainly not her real name. I wish I did. She called herself Beryl Carpenter.

That's what I'm here for. Can't you remember who it was you sold this gun to?'

'To start with I don't know that I did sell that individual gun. I sold one, certainly; but Davis & Foster must handle a good many.'

Lawson nodded, 'Quite right. We've got to check 'em all. And we shall in time. Don't worry about that.'

'I'm not worried, Inspector. Why should I be worried? Are you suggesting that I had anything to do with the bank raid in Amminster?'

'Now, don't take me up wrong, Mr Venning. I never suggested anything of the sort. And you know I didn't.'

'I may as well tell you, Inspector. I don't trust police inquiries. But if you are suspecting me —'

'I haven't said a word about suspecting you, or anybody else for that matter.'

'— I think I can put your mind at rest on that point at least. What date did you say the bank raid was?'

'Friday April the twenty-third.'

Venning drew a slim blue diary from his pocket and consulted it.

'On Wednesday April the twenty-first I flew BEA from Heathrow to Algiers. I stayed at the Hotel Bristol there for a week and flew back on the following Wednesday. If you don't believe that —'

'Why shouldn't I believe it, Mr Venning?'

'— you can check my bookings with BEA and my stay at the hotel.'

Which is exactly what I shall do, the inspector thought, but aloud he said, 'All I want from you, Mr Venning, is a bit of help if you can give it me. I want to know who you sold this gun to?'

Venning fell into one of his silences, staring almost vacantly at the inspector.

His stare might seem vacant. His mind was busy enough.

He was thinking, 'young, good-looking, well spoken'; he

124

thought he remembered, too, that Barbara had spoken to him about horses and riding ... this was just the sort of escapade the man she was living with might get up to ...

'We don't keep a record of people we sell things to,' he said finally.

'No names or addresses?'

'Not if somebody walks into the shop, pays cash and walks out with the goods under their arms.'

'And you can't remember this sale at all?'

Venning seemed to be considering. 'No, I'm afraid I can't,' he said at length. 'I can tell you the date I sold the gun, of course.'

Inspector Lawson had to be content with that ...

Three days later the inspector was discussing the case with his sergeant, back after a week's leave.

'Birmingham are getting busy on the half dozen that went up there,' he said, 'and we shall hear from them in due course.'

The sergeant knew his Lawson.

'But you don't think that's the answer?' he said.

'No, I don't. I feel sure that what we want is down here. In the south. In London. You can't explain these things logically but you get the feeling. Every Jack knows it. A particular place, a particular person – somehow you get a feeling about them. You think hallo, *there's something here*.

'That's how I felt when I went into this Toovey place.'

'You reckon what's his name, the man there, is a villain?'

'I doubt it. He certainly didn't do the job at Amminster because he's got a cast-iron alibi which I've checked with BEA and Interpol. And he's got no form. CRO know nothing about him. I got a splendid set of dabs off the gun when he had finished handling it and, like I say, no joy from CRO.

'No, I don't think he's a villain; not in our sense of the word. But he doesn't like us. He as good as told me that straight out. And it could be—' the inspector's voice trailed away. 'I don't know,' he concluded. 'All I say is I got the message that there was something about that Toovey place. If I was one of these diviners I'd say the rod twitched in my hand when I was there, but what it was trying to tell me I'm hanged if I know.

XII

Peter Venning was vastly intrigued and amused by the detective inspector's visit. So much so that shortly after Lawson left he locked the door and hung the 'Closed' notice in it.

There was still a full hour to go before he normally shut, but he wanted to sit in the back and think over what he had heard, quietly and undisturbed.

There was nothing that he didn't remember about the gun which had been shown to him. Davis & Foster's representative had introduced the dummies as a new line and had suggested that he might like to take a dozen or so to add to his already considerable spread of theatrical props.

Venning hadn't been particularly keen on the idea, but he did a fair amount of business with Davis & Foster and they could always be relied upon to treat him reasonably if he had difficulty in settling his account strictly in time.

In the end, therefore, and as part of a larger order, he had taken six of the guns and so far he had sold only one of them.

This fact didn't worry him unduly, Tooveys was not a shop which relied on a quick turnover, and he had reasonable hopes that the remaining five would go in time.

Meanwhile he had no doubts at all about the purchaser of the one gun which he had sold; and the possibilities which as yet were only vaguely forming in his mind intrigued him immensely.

At least half his pleasure in the situation came from the fact that he knew something which the police were obviously keen to find out, and he had no intention of telling them.

That same evening of the inspector's visit Venning took himself to the local public library and made somewhat tentative inquiries about the chances of looking up old files of daily newspapers.

He had never previously used the public library and had only a general idea that it included a reference service.

The range of potted information available and the cheerful willingness of people to help him in looking for it amazed him.

Within only a few minutes he was sitting at a table with *Daily Telegraph* files covering the last week of April and the first two weeks of May by his side.

While reading he remembered vaguely that he had noticed references to the Amminster bank robbery at the time; but as bank robberies, hi-jackings, ransoms for kidnapping and the like go these days it had not rated very highly, and the feature of the case which had most tended to keep it alive had been the 'au pair' slant.

This particular aspect of it had had no appeal whatever for Venning (whose interest in girls was minimal anyway) and the whole matter had lost all attraction for him as a news item after the first reading.

Now, however, he began to think that the au pair business might turn out to be extremely interesting, and his ingrained love of mystery and intrigue was whetted delightfully.

He read, and re-read, all the *Telegraph* accounts of the affair and subsequent references to its side issues slowly and carefully.

In sober fact there wasn't a great deal.

In essence it boiled down to the fact that Barrolds bank had been robbed of some twenty-seven thousand pounds; that a so-called au pair girl had been a partner in the robbery; and that the police were 'following up various lines of inquiry'.

But three facts Venning was able to note:

1. The au pair girl called herself Beryl Carpenter.
2. She was fond of horses.
3. The car used in the robbery was a Volvo.

Beryl Carpenter, Barbara Courlander – Venning wondered. He remembered distinctly that when she was working for him Barbara had more than once spoken of her liking for riding; and he thought he remembered her saying once that the man she was living with drove a Volvo.

Thus it came about that two days after Inspector Lawson's visit to Tooveys Muriel Benson, slightly surprised to hear a ring on the bell at half past two in the afternoon, went to open the front door of 'Wenlock'.

She saw a middle-aged, corpulent man who, when he wanted to, could smile pleasantly enough. He did so now.

'Mrs Benson I believe?'

'Yes?'

'Mrs Benson, I hope you will agree to help me. I have been commissioned to write a series of articles for an American magazine on the whole question of au pair girls in England —'

'Oh, I see —'

'– and, of course, after your experience our readers would be very much interested in what you have to say about it.'

'Well, it's true I did have a very unhappy experience —'

Another pleasant smile. 'I'm sure you did.'

'But really I've told the papers all about it already.'

'But not the American magazines.'

'No: there wasn't anybody from America —'

'It's a survey on the whole question of au pairs in England. The snags and dangers as well as the advantages. If you could spare me ten minutes —'

'Yes I can do that, I expect. If you like to come in I can tell you just what I told the other newspaper people, if that's what you want.'

Peter Venning said it was exactly what he wanted; and

with an inward smirk of triumph at the easiness of the first step he followed into the painfully conventional lounge.

The banker's wife found it agreeably easy to tell her whole story again, especially to a new and obviously receptive audience.

Directly after the robbery all her bridge-circle and tea-party friends were agog to listen to anything she had to tell them about it; but in reality she had very little to say, and by the time they had heard her say it half a dozen times interest began to wane very markedly.

Muriel Benson and her moans about the incredible duplicity of one who had seemed to be the perfect au pair became a bore.

'Oh, Muriel, not all that *again*,' an exasperated acquaintance who wanted to get the cards cut and dealt exclaimed; and Mrs Benson had shut up like a clam, dismayed.

... they don't want to hear about it any more, she thought, *I'm a bore ...*

Now there was somebody sympathetic, who didn't seem to find it boring at all, who apparently wanted to hear it all. Who seemed particularly interested (as Muriel Benson herself was) in the personality of the deceitful Beryl Carpenter.

'She was so nice, Mr Lamming.' (Venning had thought it easier and more convincing not to remain entirely anonymous).

'I'm sure she was.'

'She was a *lady*, Mr Lamming, a *lady*.' Mrs Benson pronounced this ultimate accolade with immense emphasis and with a great air of injured dignity: *I had no idea a lady could behave like that,* she seemed to be implying; *as one lady to another I trusted her and she let us ladies down ...*

'And she was attractive to look at?'

'Oh very.'

'A small girl, was she?'

'Oh dear me, no. Quite the reverse. Beryl was tall. Of course I'm on the short side, I know. My hubby' (Venning winced) 'jokes about it occasionally; but Beryl must have been three or four inches taller than me.'

'Dark? Fair? What did she look like?'

'Oh, she was dark.' (A great number of Muriel Benson's sentences started with the word 'Oh' which she made to sound like a mild expression of astonishment that the questioner didn't know the answer already and should have found it necessary to ask.) 'Definitely dark. Sort of Spanish-looking almost at times. I used to think she looked a bit *mysterious*.

'Once or twice I said to her – I got to know her very well, you see. At least I thought I did. We became friends – once or twice I said to her, "Beryl I'm sure you've had an interesting life. You're a bit of a mystery —" '

'And what did she say to that?'

'Oh, she just laughed. She never said anything about herself, never. I did think that was a bit strange occasionally, I must admit; but I didn't dream it was because she was mixed up in anything wrong. I tell you why I thought it was, Mr Lamming, I thought it was because she had had an unhappy love affair and had taken this post on, away in the country here, to get over it.'

Venning nodded. 'That's quite possible I suppose,' he said.

'Oh, it *is* possible. I'm sure I'm right about it too, because of what happened at the Gymkhana.'

'What was that?'

Muriel Benson gave a graphic account of the open sports car speeding by with the four gay young people one of whom shouted out, '*Hallo Barbara what brings you here?*'

Venning listened in fascinated silence.

'It wasn't "*Beryl*" he called out, but "*Barbara*". I heard him distinctly. I asked her about it a bit later – well, I didn't want to be nosey but it was definitely intriguing wasn't it?'

'Very.'

'And she said yes, it was her name in a way. She had

131

been christened Beryl Barbara and she didn't like "Barbara" but this young man did, he was Freddie somebody, and he always called her by it.'

'Fancy that,' Venning said, falling pretty neatly (he congratulated himself) into the 'Wenlock' idiom.

All the way back to London he purred inwardly with satisfaction and amusement at the success of his little game.

He liked clever little games of deception ... And who knows, he thought, it might well be developed into a bigger game yet ...

He turned over in his fertile brain the knowledge he had managed to establish already and wondered what could be made of it ...

Obviously Beryl Carpenter was Barbara Courlander; that was clear.

Barbara going as an au pair to a small house in Amminster just made no sense at all, except for the fact that the local bank manager lived there.

Evidently, then, it was a carefully-thought-out job with Barbara's current man no doubt at the back of it.

Venning considered the question of Barbara Courlander. He very clearly remembered her coming into the shop, out of the blue, and asking if there was a job going.

Attractive (not that women, qua women, had much appeal for him, but he could see the quality of attraction in a woman; smell it; even be a little revolted by it in a fascinated way) attractive then, and business-like.

She had undeniably been a success in the shop, and in those days had seemed glad enough of the money he paid her.

But he had never liked her; and this was largely because, despite surface politeness which was assumed between them to make contact in daily matters easier, he was well aware that Barbara in turn had never liked him.

Peter Venning had origins which he kept very much in the background.

In these brave days of depressing equality nobody is supposed to mind who anybody else's parents are, or where anybody else comes from. The fact remains that a lot of people still care a very great deal if they think that other people have been luckier in those things than themselves. An inferiority complex is still one of the most destructive cankers that can eat away inside a man.

Attractive and efficient in the shop Barbara proved to be; and besides that *a stuck-up bitch* Venning had soon found himself thinking.

He thought she despised him and he hated her for it.

He also thought that at times she was slightly scared of him and he found that pleasing.

On the few occasions when her efficiency slipped up a little (nearly always in the matter of the code) he didn't miss the chance of pointing it out to her.

'It must be marvellous, Barbara dear, to be as well off as you and not to have to worry about the odd ten pounds.'

'I'm never quite sure about that damned code.'

'Unfortunately I have to be. We haven't all got expectations from rich old gentlemen dying. What a very comforting star you have hitched yourself to, haven't you, dear?'

She hadn't liked that. Which pleased him; he hadn't meant her to like it.

When she was getting ready to leave that evening, tying a red scarf round that dark hair, Venning said, 'Going a bit early, aren't you?'

Barbara bent slightly to get a better view in the inadequate mirror that hung in the minute so-called 'office'.

'I often stay on late so you've nothing to grumble about,' she answered, 'and I'm leaving early because I'm going out this evening to a party with the man I've hitched myself up to, as you call it.'

'What do you call it?'

'I call it living with him. A man living with a woman. But I don't suppose you would know about that, would you?'

The sallow flabby face flushed slightly.

'Look, dear, if you are going to turn nasty I can turn nasty too, you know.'

He spoke the words softly but with venom and when her eyes met his he thought that for a moment she looked slightly scared.

Nothing more was said because Mrs Todd, the cleaning woman, came in to do her 'evening hour'; but it had come into Venning's mind then, and now on the way back from Amminster it came back to him with renewed force, that someday he might be in a position to make the stuck-up bitch really scared . . .

XIII

'Good evening,' Peter Venning said in his smooth, soft voice. He ran an appreciative eye over her. 'That gold lamé suits you to perfection.'

That's one thing to be said for Peter Venning's sort, Barbara thought, they do notice what a woman is wearing and if they like it they say nice things about it.

'Good heavens, you! I thought you must be a Jehovah's Witness, or canvassing for some local election or other.'

Venning smiled. 'No. Just your ex-employer. May I come in for a moment?'

Barbara led the way into the living-room stirred now by agreeable curiosity.

In her mind Peter Venning equated naturally with antiques, and since she was now launched in the antique world with Stella Margerrison and their venture was already proving surprisingly successful, and since she was pretty certain that the gossip of the trade would have brought this news to Venning's ears, she had a shrewd suspicion that some sort of deal might be in the offing. A merger of the two businesses perhaps? Or even an offer to go back to him at Tooveys again, but as partner this time on equal terms. A number of possible explanations of his visit half formed, were vaguely considered, and dissolved again in her mind.

Half-formed and vague they might be; but they were all pleasant. They had the flavour of success about them. They meant that Peter, the sarcastic old bastard, realised that she was making good.

She had never liked Venning, and even in the euphoria of success she wasn't now fooling herself that she had; but in the daily affairs of running the shop they had got on well enough – each had had the sense to arrange that they *did* get on well enough, things being pleasanter that way – and whatever you might think about the man as a person you had to admit that he knew his business.

'You're going out?' he asked.

She extended her left hand, the nails still not quite dry. 'War paint.'

He knew about these things, of course. Masculine men, Vyvyan for instance, tended to like the results but to be blissfully ignorant of the means that achieved them. She thought of Vyvyan for a moment. Dewsbury hadn't he said? Somewhere up in the far north. The eh-by-gum country. Drinking too much, almost certainly. Barbara was a firm believer in the complete necessity of drink as a cushion against the buffets of life; but even she thought that Vyvyan had been overdoing it a bit lately. Stupid to drink till you become stupid. A self-evident truth, that, she thought ... a platitude ... God, I'm becoming platitudinous now; and certainly Vyvyan is; he has lost his *oomph*; I haven't lost mine; I've got (correction: *we*'ve got) twenty-seven thousand pounds and I've got my *oomph* ...

'Mr Weighman's not in?' Venning asked.

'I'm expecting someone to call for me.'

He assessed her tone of voice correctly.

'Not Mr Weighman?'

'I'm expecting someone to call for me.'

'Then I shall be in the way, and that would never do, of course, would it? Immediately?'

She glanced at the ormulu clock.

'In twenty minutes.'

'I hear you are still interested in the antique world,' he said.

Barbara smiled and inwardly was considerably gratified; it looked as though her guess was coming true.

'Who told you that?' she asked. She knew precisely what

his answer would be and he didn't disappoint her; he used the exact phrase she had already mentally prescribed for him.

'Oh, a little bird.' His eye moved to the corner table. 'Can I have a drink?'

'Of course. What would you like?'

'A Bloody Mary.'

Barbara mixed two Bloody Marys and, fingernails now dry, brought his over to him.

'What interests you about my still being in the antique world?' she asked.

'With Lady Margerrison, isn't it?'

'With Stella Margerrison, that's right.'

'Ah, of course, you know all these titled people by their Christian names, don't you?'

'A lot of them,' Barbara said complacently, amused that she could touch the old sore spot so quickly and so surely.

'We are doing quite nicely,' she added.

'So I hear.'

'And how is Tooveys doing?'

'I'm thinking of leaving Tooveys.'

This surprised Barbara. All the time she had been at Tooveys sales had always kept up well and (in spite of an occasional lapse on her part over the code) nothing was ever sold at a loss.

'Leaving?' she queried.

'I don't want to. It's established and I've worked up a good connection there and although one has one's rather thin patches, on the whole I wasn't doing badly.'

'Come off it, Peter. You were making a nice little fortune there.'

The flabby face creased into a smile, the heavy eyes half closed for a moment as though at some inward humorous reflection.

'Oh, that's your extravagant way of speaking, dear, isn't it? Some people make fortunes so quickly and so easily

137

don't they, nowadays?'

'But what do you want to leave for?'

'I'm afraid you don't listen very carefully, do you? I just said a moment ago that I *don't* want to leave. That's to say I don't *want* to, but I've simply got to. It's these sharks of landlords. The lease comes to an end next September and I've been offered a renewal for seven years, and do you know what the man is asking? —'

Barbara said she hadn't a clue; and with one of the smiles which she had long ago learnt to mistrust Venning said he was surprised to hear her say that as he was quite sure that she was very well up in money matters.

'You always did enjoy being sarcastic, didn't you, Peter?'

'Immensely. It's one of the more refined pleasures of life. We are not going to have one of our little tiffs dear, are we?'

'Why should we?'

'Why indeed? I was telling you about the lease. If I take up the renewal I shall have to pay an additional three thousand a year; on top, that is, of the rent I'm already paying. Well, it just isn't on. I'm afraid I said something rather rude to the landlord about his lease and I started to look elsewhere and to think of other possibilities.'

... one of which, Barbara thought, was what he is pretty obviously going to suggest any moment now: the idea of joining up with Stella Margerrison and myself ...

She would want time to think the suggestion over and to discuss it with Stella who might be entirely opposed to it; but she could see certain advantages in it. Peter Venning had a good deal of knowledge and he would bring a considerable ready made clientele with him ...

'And I think I've found one,' Venning continued.

'Such as?'

'I've found a house in Sussex. Right out in the country. It's an old mill house and it would make a marvellous place for selling antiques. Of course it's a bit off the map but in these days when every Tom, Dick and Harry has a motor-car that doesn't matter so much. In fact it's something of an advantage, people go exploring the lanes and by-ways and come across your shop tucked away there and they are so pleased at making what they think is a wonderful discovery that often enough you can sell them almost anything, and stick the price on pretty steeply, too!'

'Sounds just right for you,' Barbara said, wondering just how she was going to phrase her reply when he went on to suggest that she should give up her alliance with Stella Margerrison and rejoin him.

'Of course I shall want some capital,' he went on. 'This place, Mill Race House it's called – rather a good name for an antique shop, don't you think – The Mill Race? – is in a frightful state. But *frightful*. Neglected isn't the word for it. There's everything to be done there; but once it is done, and I've already had an architect to look at it and he sees *immense* possibilities, once it is done up the result will be quite something.

'But, as I say, that needs capital. I shall have to spend quite a lot on it. I want some money. I was wondering if you would like to come in with me —'

He let the sentence die away in the air and watched her reaction to it. By the expression on his face you might have thought that he was finding the situation more amusing than anything else.

'You mean come in as a partner?'

'I didn't say anything about "partner", did I, dear? I mean lend me five thousand pounds at a very, *very* nominal rate of interest.'

Barbara stared at him in astonishment; but she was prevented from having to find any answer by the ringing of the front door bell.

'– Ah, your friend. I mustn't be in the way, must I? If he wants to know who I am, just say I came on a business visit.' He rose and moved towards the door, turning to explode his hitherto concealed landmine.

'Well, it is business in a way, isn't it? I've been having some very tiresome inquiries lately about that gun you came in and bought from me. For amateur theatricals you said it was, didn't you?'

God Almighty, Barbara thought, *so that's it*; that's what the cunning bastard has got up his sleeve all the time; he knows something . . . he can't *know*; but he suspects something . . .

She watched him narrowly and fear showed in her eyes. Seeing it there Venning began to enjoy himself enormously . . . the stuck-up bitch would soon be finding out that she didn't hold all the cards in her hand. Not by a long chalk. And it would be fun making her realise the fact . . .

Barbara managed to keep her voice reasonably under control as she asked, as casually as she could. 'Who was asking you about it?'

'I don't think he was particularly interested in antiques or theatre props,' Venning said. 'Actually he turned out to be a policeman, a detective.'

Barbara half turned away and put her glass down carefully on a side table. Try as she might she could not keep her hand steady as she did so.

'What an extraordinary thing,' she said. 'What did you tell him?'

To let her have a small foretaste of what sweating it out would be like Venning took his time over selecting and lighting a cigarette.

Then, the first satisfied pull of smoke floating in the air, he smiled and said, 'I told him I simply couldn't remember a thing about it – but I did wonder why he, *they*, wanted to know.'

The front door bell rang again, impatiently this time.

Venning was all mock apologies . . . 'Now I really must go; who am I to stand in the way of a romantic evening?' he laughed.

At the door he turned and, his voice hardening just a little, said, 'Perhaps you could come round one day and have a talk about it in the shop. *Soon.*'

XIV

Barbara's first reaction was thank God Charles is taking me out this evening; she didn't want to spend an evening alone in the flat mulling over what the sarcastic (and now dangerous?) Peter Venning had said, and left unsaid, to her. Just exactly his cup of tea, a situation like that; just exactly the situation his sort would enjoy. The position of all power and no danger. Well, that might have to be looked into she thought; not that you can immediately think very clearly or in any detail when something like that has just been sprung on you. In the last sentence, too. Typical that. The exit line with the bite in it 'perhaps' (perhaps!) 'you could come round one day and have a talk about it in the shop. *Soon.*'

Even if she had had anything ready to reply to that there wasn't time to say it before she had to open the door to let Charles in. Charles who had rung twice and was just about to press the bell again. His Lordship wasn't used to being kept waiting. Peter Venning, trust him, behaved adroitly when the door opened. He slid out making conventional noises of polite departure and disappeared into the night before Barbara had to begin to worry about introductions.

'Charles, how nice to see you.'

'I was beginning to think you weren't in. Who was that feller?'

'I used to know him in the antiques world and he came round to try to sell me something.'

'A picture?' (Charles, rather unexpectedly, was genuinely interested in paintings.)

'No. More an idea really.'

'You going to buy it?'

'I'm thinking it over. Probably not, on the whole.'

Charles was large, portly, fresh complexioned, a very well preserved fifty-five; he sported a moustache which, had he been prominent enough to be in the range of the cartoonists, would have been a godsend to them.

Mixing drinks for them (she had another Bloody Mary, he his usual stiff whisky) Barbara felt a renewal of her first reaction of gratitude that she was going to spend the evening with him and not alone. Charles was predictable and uncomplicated. Much easier to deal with than that bastard Venning who was unpredictable, you never knew what he would be up to next, except you could be pretty certain that it would be something unpleasant and complicated; you couldn't tell in what devious way his nancy-boy mind would delight to work. Charles's incipient irritation at having been kept waiting on the doorstep was soon assuaged. Malt does more than Milton can to justify God's ways to man. A good malt whisky did a great deal to justify the general condition and conduct of the world in Charles's eyes.

A simple fellow in many ways, this man of country acres and responsibilities. Both faithfully looked after and discharged. A user of Old Spice after shave lotion which, since he always shaved immediately before taking a lady out in the evening, was subtly but agreeably noticeable. Barbara enjoyed seeing him in the small living-room in Hambledon Street; maybe a shade too large and ruddy-complexioned to look absolutely at home there, but nevertheless in his own way impressive. Caution had hitherto precluded his coming there, but with Vyvyan safely anchored in the heavy wool part of the world caution had for once been relaxed. He's a jealous devil. Barbara had more than once explained, as jealous as hell. Charles had puffed out approving cheeks, a habit of his when making pontifical utterances and said so he ought to be. Quite right. The male animal defends his territory and his female. Law of nature. Like birds. Quite right to be jealous, what? He must be one of the few remaining Englishmen who really did bark out an aggressively interrogative *what*? at the end of every third or fourth sentence, thought Barbara. The habit rather endeared him to her, as an eccentricity in some large domestic pet – say an Old English sheepdog – might. *Charles and his what.* A saying which almost instantly, of course, became charged with double meaning and the source of much hilarity between them, because, when not sitting in the family pew in the parish church, walking magisterially over the home farm, or taking the chair at the annual meeting of the local Conservative branch, this said Charles was a mighty seducer before the Lord and a great performer in bed. Which was one of the reasons, perhaps the main one, why Barbara enjoyed her affair with him. There were other, secondary, ones. As for instance that even in these days of coronets being deliberately dragged down among the weeds there was still an undeniable satisfaction in being mistress to a duke. And, again, Charles reminded Barbara of her own father. Allowing for certain differences in scale of living and background there was a distinct similarity.

Fellings had certainly not been ducal in extent, but it had not been a semi-detached villa either. It had been an establishment. An establishment run and ruined by Barbara's mother. The servants, there were far too many of them anyway, were always changing because they couldn't stand her temper; the bank manager was always writing warning letters because he couldn't stand her extravagances. What Barbara remembered mostly, after her mother's unpredictable tantrums and her father's Olympian aloofness, was Nannie Haynes. Nannie Haynes presiding in the nursery. Nannie Haynes making toast and Marmite for tea; or blackcurrant syrup when any of the four children had winter colds. Nannie Haynes was the one unchanging element in Fellings. To consider getting rid of her would have been an act of supreme folly that even Barbara's wayward and tempestuous mother didn't contemplate it.

Individual incidents stood out in the flashback of memory: the time when Barbara's mother flourishing a riding crop chased her youngest son, aged six, along the broad terrace all round the house furious with him because he had shown fear in the hunting field; the moment when, after some display of childish perverseness, Nannie Haynes had folded her to an ample bosom and said *Barbie, Barbie if you go on like this you'll never come to any good will you, my chick* ...

A prophecy not wholly justified, Barbara now thought totting up her achievements: a share in a highly desirable flat in Hambledon Street, S.W.3; a Duke, no less, just embarking on his second large whisky in the living-room of the said flat, shortly to take her out to dinner (at the Ecu de France she hoped) and then subsequently to make love to her; an agreeable job in a world she liked with a woman she liked; twenty-seven thousand pounds in notes stacked away in suitcases in the glory-hole; and, of course, on the debit side, that bastard Venning.

Barbara, her third Bloody Mary keeping pace with Charles's second whisky, decided that something would have to be done about Venning. *Barbara isn't afraid*, her mother had shouted belabouring her terrified son with the riding crop, *why the devil are you afraid, your sister isn't* ...

Of course it wasn't true that she wasn't afraid; even at that age she had realised that grown-ups usually got things slightly wrong. She *was* afraid. But in a curious way which she couldn't explain she enjoyed being afraid. Danger put an edge on living. In a way she was afraid of Peter Venning; in her worst thoughts about the pale-faced, flabby, soft-spoken man she could imagine him practising every sort of black art and diabolical dealing, but this wouldn't prevent her doing something about him if he made too much of a nuisance of himself. And enjoy doing it. Which was where Vyvyan was letting her down, she reflected. He had been brilliant thinking up and working out the Amminster business, and now, all of a sudden, the steam seemed to have gone out of him. He was drinking too much, of course. Not that she objected strongly to that unless it made other delights impracticable. A great deal of it was done, as far as she could make out, in the Bombardier. The Bombardier seemed to have an altogether odd effect on him. Was there somebody there, she occasionally wondered. Did he have a daily assignation there? Or had he fallen for some dewy-eyed luscious creature behind the bar? I must go and have a look one day, she thought. Meanwhile she had her duke who had a healthy ducal appetite for his nosebag (as he was wont to describe his dinner) and other delights.

'Where's it to be? The Ecu?'

'The Ecu would be marvellous, Charles.'

'Let's get cracking, then. We don't want to spoil a good dinner by hurrying; on the other hand we want to give ourselves plenty of time afterwards, what?'

Nosebags at the Ecu turned out to be exquisite *caneton à l'orange.*

'The man who doesn't care about what he eats is a fool,' Charles said towards the end of the meal, 'and usually a dull dog into the bargain. Johnson said something to that effect.'

'Johnson?'

'Doctor Samuel.'

'I didn't know you were a man of letters, Charles.'

'I'm not. Nor was Johnson really. He could ride as well as the biggest rogue in England. Somebody said that about him on the South Downs. Horses are the dividing line. If a man rides he may be a knave; he probably is; but he's a good sort of knave. There's something about him. He's on the way to salvation.'

Barbara was greatly amused by this. 'Are you on your way to salvation, Charles?'

A warm hand gripped her thigh. 'We're on our way to bed. Drink up your coffee, what?'

Barbara was returned in style (in the Town Rolls driven

by the inscrutable Mont) to Hambledon Street at nine o'clock the following morning. Charles, summoned by landlordly duties, had caught the eight-thirty from Paddington for the West Country.

'Quite a night, what?' was his leave-taking, which Barbara rightly construed as a recommendation of her prowess.

During dinner at the Ecu and the subsequent proceedings she had been able, after the defensive self-deluding fashion of humans, to persuade herself – *almost* to persuade herself – of a number of comforting things about the Peter Venning situation. Such as that he was bluffing; that he couldn't possibly know anything about Amminster; that she only had to brazen it out, etc., etc. At one or two moments of extra activity on Charles's part she was even able to half believe that Peter Venning didn't really exist and that if she simply refused to bother about him he would conveniently fade away.

At nine o'clock next morning, entering an empty flat, these protective layers of self-deception were no longer any use. The chill east wind of the morning after and the day ahead blew searchingly through them.

The telephone was ringing as she went in through the front door.

Vyvyan. From the wild and woolly north.

And Vyvyan in a bad temper. No unusual occurrence with him these days.

'Where the hell have you been? I tried to get you at eleven and at half past last night. And I tried again at eight o'clock this morning —'

'I never answer the telephone before nine. You ought to know that.'

'I suppose you have been in the flat some time during the night have you?'

'If you must know —'

'I'm not particularly interested. Don't tell me.'

147

'– if you must know I went to the ballet with Stella Margerrison. She had two tickets for *Giselle*. Two marvellous. What time will you be back?'

'Not till tomorrow now. Possibly the day after. The managing director up here wants to see me. He's been delayed flying back from Sweden and they want me to hang on here till he comes.'

Barbara excited from the conversation with some conventionally silly remark about not knowing how the Bombardier would get on without him, but she replaced the telephone receiver thoughtfully.

She had been looking forward to Vyvyan's return so that she could discuss the Venning situation with him; but on reflection she began to think that it might be better if she did the preliminary skirmishing herself.

If the two men met Vyvyan – who would probably be at least semi-tight – would almost certainly lose his temper, a circumstance which Venning would enjoy and one which wouldn't help in any way.

. . . the truth about Vyvyan, she thought as she went about the flat on minor household chores, was that he had lost his edge . . . *give me the knife*; she appreciated Lady Macbeth's dilemma and entirely approved of her solution for it, *give me the knife* . . .

Half past two had always tended to be a slack time at Tooveys and so Barbara contrived that it was just about then that she turned out of Sloane Square, which looked gay and lively in the afternoon sunshine, and went up the three shallow steps into the shop.

A customer was talking with Venning.

An American. Barbara, who had learnt to be pretty good on American accents, put him down as Boston, rich, knowledgeable and civilised. He was in fact all of these things.

He inquired the price of the pair of silver Georgian candelabra that had taken his fancy.

When Venning, who regarded rich silver-seeking Americans as a special sort of manna provided by heaven for his own particular benefit, quoted an utterly outrageous figure the Bostonian smiled in a gentle way and said, 'Ah, is that perhaps a special figure that you keep for us ignorant Americans?'

As this was precisely the case Venning became indignant and blustered, 'I hope you are not suggesting, er . . .'

The Bostonian bid him a courteous afternoon and left the shop.

Venning watched him go and then took his time about turning his attention to Barbara. There was an expression on his face which Barbara didn't like; it reminded her of some bit of poetry, a jingle, which should have come into her head but didn't . . .

'I hope you enjoyed your night out,' he began.

'I usually manage to enjoy an evening out.'

'And in very distinguished company —'

'*Spider,*' Barbara remembered the jingle. '*Will you walk into my parlour said the spider to the fly.*'

An admirable piece of casting Peter Venning as the fat, pallid life-sucking spider; but she hadn't any intention of supplying the part of the fly . . .

'. . . *very* distinguished,' Venning was continuing, 'Didn't I recognise somebody right out of Debrett?'

'I don't know how many people you know out of Debrett, so I can't say if you would recognise any of them.'

He didn't like that. He wasn't meant to like it. Barbara knew his little vanities and weaknesses well enough. When she had said it she regretted having done so. No point in riling the bastard before they began discussion . . . the sort of stupid thing Vyvyan would do . . . I'll let him do the talking, she thought, and play along with him a bit . . .

There was silence.

The Spider obviously didn't propose to start the talking. He was well satisfied not to. She had been sweating it out for less than twenty-four hours and already had felt the compulsion to come and see him. Let her start then. He waited.

'I'm sorry our talk got interrupted last night,' she said at last.

'Naturally when somebody out of Debrett comes to see you I have to go.'

Barbara felt like telling him for God's sake drop all this silly inverted snobbery; it just doesn't belong to this day and age, so for Pete's sake start acting and talking naturally – if you can – and we might get somewhere.

But she didn't want to quarrel with him – yet.

'This place you were talking about in Sussex, the Mill Race didn't you call it? I think that's a marvellous name for an antique shop.'

He nodded; but he didn't say anything.

'And you say it will cost quite a bit to do it up and so on?'

'You must come and look at it and give me your opinion about how that five thousand pounds can be best spent.'

'Five thousand pounds?'

'The five thousand pounds that crept into our conversation towards the end yesterday evening. Do you remember? The five thousand pounds you are going to lend me, well I did say at a very low rate of interest, but thinking it over (and I'm sure you've been doing that too) it will be free of all interest, won't it? Just a nice straightforward friendly loan.'

'Suppose there was such a loan when would you be able to repay it?'

The Spider laughed. Unpleasantly yet with some show of genuine amusement. He was enjoying himself.

'You do keep up pretences well, don't you?' he said. 'There isn't going to be any repayment, dear. I know it and you know it. Just five thousand pounds. In notes. A friendly gesture to help me start up a new place.'

They had moved into the small 'office' that led out of the

150

back of the shop proper and were sitting in its confined space on either side of the minute gas-fire which in that sunless recess Venning kept going most days of the year.

He stretched a hand out to move a pile of newspapers which were stacked sufficiently near the fire to be in danger of scorching.

Extravagant possibilities began to run at the back of Barbara's mind as she watched him ... the place was so old and dry it would go up like tinder if a fire *did* start ... if a fire could be induced to start ... but then of course it wasn't Tooveys she wanted to get rid of ... he would have to be in the fire somehow and incapable of getting out ... drugged? drunk? insensible? ...

'Mustn't burn the place down,' he said, moving the papers to safety, 'even if I am leaving it.'

'No, you mustn't do that.'

'What a funny little woman Mrs Benson is,' Venning continued lightly. 'Not your type at all, I would have thought. You *must* have been bored there.'

... so it wasn't all guesswork. He knew; and knew a good deal apparently. Certainly knew all he needed in order to be dangerous. All right, she thought, the cards were on the table now, but she wasn't going to let him get any joy out of it if she could help it ...

'Actually I wasn't bored at all. I rather enjoyed the whole thing.'

'I believe you would. I can believe that. Well, we have to pay for our enjoyments don't we? Isn't that what the moralists tell us? Five thousand pounds.'

Barbara kept silent for a few seconds and then said, 'I suppose you have heard of the word "blackmail"?'

Venning laughed our loud. 'Now you are coming up to expectations. I am really enjoying this now. Blackmail, my dear Barbara, in case you don't know, is the demanding of money by threats of some kind.

'Who is demanding money from you? Not I. I'm not demanding anything. We worked together in the antiques business and are still friends I hope; and so, knowing that you have come in for a bit of good luck lately – what fun you must have had with that au pair nonsense – I am suggesting that you might be good enough to help me with a loan. And threats? Who's threatening anybody? I wouldn't dream of threatening you. Especially with all the high-powered friends you've got.'

Barbara studied him, her mind as she did so a cinematograph screen on which a dozen half formed, half realised images flashed, superimposed, dissolved. Eventually she nodded slowly.

'You want to get a rewrite job done on your dialogue,' she advised him. 'All that innocent babe stuff is so corny. Still, like you say, you're enjoying it. O.K., you go on enjoying yourself. And what happens if I find I can't manage this loan you talk about?'

'I've got a very peculiar sort of memory. Now, the other day when that detective asked me could I remember who I sold the gun to I said no I was sorry I couldn't, my mind was a blank about it. Well, something might occur to you, he said, do your best to think it over and let me know if you come up with anything. So, of course, if anything *did* occur to me about it I shall have to let him know shouldn't I?'

Barbara was silent for some seconds. Then she said, 'You want five thousand pounds?'

'In notes.'

'I shall have to talk this over —'

'With Mr Weighman. Naturally. I see that. I want you to talk it over.'

'He'll think what I think – that it's blackmail.'

'Oh dear, you have got that word on the brain, haven't you? Your Mr Weighman is a businessman, isn't he? I really can't see him going round to the local police station and saying three months ago I and my girl-friend lifted twenty-seven thousand pounds out of Barrolds bank in

Amminster and now we are having trouble with a pal about how the money should be split up, please will you help us. As I say, I can't see him going round to the C.I.D. with that tale, can you?'

After another short silence Barbara asked, 'If we talk it over and agree to this, when do you want the money by?'

The Spider smiled.

'You always were a sensible girl,' he said. 'No point in dragging things out is there? If I haven't heard from you in a week at the outside I've a feeling my memory is going to start stirring, and you don't want that to happen, do you?'

Vyvyan parked the Volvo half on the pavement, half in the street and let himself into the flat more than glad to have the long tiring drive from Yorkshire behind him.

Barbara wasn't in and he found himself glad that she wasn't. At the same time he was wryly conscious of it being odd that he should feel like that. Something had gone wrong ... ever since that business at Amminster, he thought, something has gone wrong. Something has gone out of it. Something has gone out of *me*. I enjoyed Amminster. Literally did enjoy planning it and doing it. And it came off. It was successful. So what's gone wrong? ...

He went at once to the drinks table in the corner and there was a layer of his consciousness in which for a moment he knew something like guilt (but warm, comforting guilt) at the relief, even the excitement, that stirred in him as his fingers closed round the whisky bottle.

Two days before he had gone up to Yorkshire Mrs Bennett in the Bombardier had broken, or at least stretched, one of the several rules by which she regulated her admirable life ... *never comment on a customers habits* ... ('Do you really think you want another one, Mr Weighman?' she asked.)

Vyvyan was astounded ... how the devil did she know his name, anyway? If any man had been careful to take ad-

vantage of the anonymity that a pub offered he had been
... but it was obviously an honour ... he found himself
curiously moved by the fact that this unusual woman should
have taken the trouble to find out who he was ...

'Yes, I am sure,' he said, putting his money on the
counter.

Mrs Bennett had already stretched her code of conduct
to the limit. Without any further comment and with an impassive face she poured out a double Scotch.

Vyvyan watched her do so, squirted his customary token
amount of soda-water into the glass then, moving over to
the window-sill, emptied the whole lot over the roots of a
pot plant standing there.

Mrs Bennett watched this dispassionately.

'I don't suppose it will do the aspidistra any good,' she
said.

'I hate bloody aspidistras, anyway,' Vyvyan told her and
walked out.

The following morning he was in at his usual time, demanding his usual drink, and carrying a large expensive
sheaf of Madame Gregoire.

For a moment even Mrs Bennett had been taken aback.
Then she smiled slightly, 'It's a long time since anyone
bought me roses,' she said.

Now, in Hambledon Street, Vyvyan took the first large
gulp of his drink; swilled the liquid round in his mouth;
swallowed it.

'*Ah.*'

This was the reassuring stuff, he thought, this helped a
man to contract out of things ... ballet? Had Barbara really
been to the ballet with Stella Margerrison? ... Probably
not ... in a book the lights would have failed in the middle
of the first act, or the prima ballerina would have been
taken ill, and Barbara, questioned, wouldn't have known
about such contretemps; all neatly and tidily worked out
... that was how books worked out; but not life; life some-

how got itself into a god-awful mess; after a while you discovered that the best you could do was to put up with things and hang on; but you also discovered that there was a private retreat where nobody could follow you and where things didn't matter ... even if the private retreat did have John Haig written on the door ... he wondered if Mrs Bennett had a private retreat in her life? ...

While he was pouring out his second glass Barbara came in. He was aware at once of something slightly different about her ... difficult to put a finger on it exactly ... somehow she seemed noisier than usual and Barbara normally was not a noisy person; there was a briskness about her, a to-hell-with-them-all air ...

'Mix one for me will you?' she said. 'If there's any left.'

Pinpricks, even sledge hammer blows, about his drinking had never worried Vyvyan much and didn't mean a thing to him these days.

'How was *Giselle?*' he asked.

'*Giselle?*'

'It's a ballet. You went to it with Stella Margerrison; if you remember.'

'Oh. *Giselle*; yes; that was all right. Fine. But I've something else to talk to you about.'

'Thank God for that. I don't really want to hear some botched-up account of what you didn't see at Covent Garden.'

Barbara laughed. An uncharacteristic brassy sort of laugh. It struck Vyvyan again that she was in an odd mood. Odd and dangerous she sounded.

'Probably not,' she said, 'but I don't know that you will be all that keen on hearing this other lot, either. Peter Venning called here yesterday.'

'Venning? The man you used to work for at Tooveys?'

'Peter Venning.'

'What did he want?'

Barbara laughed again. 'Five thousand pounds.'

155

Vyvyan looked blank. 'Why on earth should Venning come here asking for five thousand quid?'

'Because he knows, *knows*, that you and I tied up little Benson and took the money out of the bank at Amminster. At least he knows that I was concerned in it.'

Vyvyan, who had been about to take another swig at his whisky slowly lowered the glass from his lips. His face had lost a good deal of its colour.

'How on earth can he know that? *Know* it?' he asked.

'The gun.'

'What about the gun.'

'The police must have picked it up and traced it somehow. Anyway a man from the C.I.D. has been at Tooveys, actually with the gun, showing it to Venning and asking him could he remember whom he sold it to.'

There was even less colour now in Vyvyan's cheeks. He was thinking of the TV documentary about Wormwood Scrubs.

'And Venning told him it was you?' he asked.

'No, he didn't. He told him he couldn't remember.'

'Why did he do that?'

'Because he wants five thousand pounds. From us. Out of our twenty-seven thousand. And then he'll keep his mouth shut. Or so he says.'

Vyvyan drained his glass and put it down thoughtfully.

'Christ Almighty,' he said at last.

Barbara watched him in almost contemptuous anger.

'There's not much point in drinking yourself stupid and saying, "*Christ Almighty*",' she said. 'Christ Almighty won't do much for us. We've got to help ourselves.'

'The perfect crime! What a fool I was.'

'It would have been perfect too, except for the gun.'

'What a typical woman's remark – flawless except for the flaw!'

'If when we were bundling Benson out of the car we hadn't somehow brushed the gun out with him —'

'We? *I* didn't brush the gun out. It must have been you.'

'For God's sake, Vyvyan, what does it matter who did it? All right, *I* did it. If it flatters your wonderful masculine vanity to say that, say it. We shall want more than masculine vanity to get us out of this mess. We shall want guts and determination. We shall want to do something.'

XV

Like all good Jacks William Lawson strongly disliked seeing a case die on his hands. Even when commonsense told him that it was ninety-nine per cent certain that a case *had* died he was still extremely loath to admit the fact either to himself or to his subordinates.

The rate of detection for burglaries in Amminster was a good one, forty-one per cent; this compared favourably with the average rate throughout England, but in his moments of depression the detective inspector had to contemplate the fact that good (by comparison) as the rate might be it still meant that nearly sixty per cent of burglaries on his patch got away with it.

This was not a comforting thought, and it was one of the reasons why the inspector hated giving up a case; there might be only one per cent chance left of solving it, but as long as that one chance in a hundred was there he refused to put the file away.

Another reason, of course, was just plain obstinacy, an indispensible requisite in his demanding job.

'Father's just so damned *pig-headed*,' his daughter Lucy complained more than once, and her mother, while feeling bound to reprimand such unfilial outspokenness, had secretly to agree; once her William started to go after a thing it took a great deal to make him give it up.

This quality of tenacity was one which the inspector looked for and encouraged in his juniors and it was one which young detective Terence Foster possessed to an admirable degree.

Occasionally Lawson would look at the mountainous piles of forms, returns, certificates and reports heaped on his desk all clamouring for instant completion and return to higher authority and wonder how in hell he and his men could be expected to be doing their real job, out and about catching villains, when they were forced to put in half their time as clerks.

Pressure of this kind of work had forced him to free his sergeant from the bank robbery case and in his place young Foster had been brought in to do the leg work.

One of the things which made the inspector popular with his men was that if you worked with him you were very largely taken into his confidence.

You were briefed about the case so that you knew as much about it as your boss did.

Put in possession of the facts in this way young Terence Foster was asked by the inspector for his views.

'Well, sir, the way I see it we ought to tackle this red sports car at the gymkhana. There was somebody in that car who knew the girl, that's certain. If we can find him we can find her.'

The inspector nodded.

'We've done quite a bit along that line, but maybe not enough.'

'You can't have done enough, sir, can you?'

'Why?'

'You haven't got the answer.'

Lawson thought I'll either sack this boy for cheekiness or promote him.

'You go and get the answer, then,' he said.

Three weeks later Foster came into the inspector's office to report progress.

'Sit down, lad, no sense in being uncomfortable.'

The young detective seated himself.

'Seen any good red sports cars lately?' Lawson asked.

'As a matter of fact I have seen one, sir; but it's not ours, I'm afraid.'

'That's not much use, then, is it?'

'I have found out one or two things, though —'

'I'm listening —'

'I started off by calling on Mrs Benson a couple of times. Not that she was much help. By the way, sir, did you know that Benson is being forcibly retired by the bank.'

'No, I didn't. Why is that?'

'They reckon he acted stupidly —'

'Well, of course he acted stupidly. But that was part of the plot, wasn't it? What age is Benson? Fifty?'

'Something like that I expect. Old, anyway.'

'Old! It won't be long before you won't be thinking of fifty as old, I can tell you. But I grant you that fifty, if that's what Benson is, is an awkward age. A dangerous age. Especially for a man like him. He's a little man who has led a sheltered domestic life.'

'Like a rabbit in a hutch.'

'That's what life is for a lot of people. So the plot was to get an attractive young woman, a sexy girl I expect she was really, established in the household and let her get to work on Benson.'

'You think he gave her a roll in the hay sir?'

'May have done. It's a common enough human diversion. But I daresay her brief would be to play up to him. Flatter him. *I think it's simply marvellous how you businessmen know all these things about money* . . . that sort of thing.

'It's a classic feminine approach and men have always fallen for it. Intelligent men, men of integrity, who would go to the stake sooner than deliberately sell the pass have only got to have a bit of flattery laid on by an admiring woman and they will do all sorts of silly things.

'From all accounts that's what Benson did; and if the bank are rapping him over the knuckles for it I'm not a bit surprised.'

'Mrs Benson wasn't much use, anyway.'

'No. I think we've sucked her dry.'

'An open car; a sports car, she calls it; four people in it,

160

two men, two girls; all youngish; and the car might (but it is only *might*) have been red.'

'So where did you go from there?'

'I went to interview Captain Praed at Terrington. He's the secretary of the hunt. I asked him about car parking and admissions and so on at the gymkhana. The arrangement is that there's only one entrance to the field and all cars had to pay to come in. A quid a go. There were two men on the gate taking the money and giving out tickets and they both belong to the British Legion. Apparently the Legion supplies these two chaps and the Hunt doesn't actually pay them individually but it makes a sizeable donation to the Legion funds. The two chaps this year were brothers, Harry and Fred Loakes —'

'Mill Lane?'

'Those are the ones, sir. I went to see them —'

'Any joy?'

'I tell you this, Inspector, if you want to get a real good comedy cabaret turn for the Police Ball sign up the Loakes brothers. One can't answer without the other; you ask Harry a question and he turns to Fred; you ask Fred and he has to consult Harry first. And whatever one says one minute the other contradicts the next.'

'They ought to stand for the Council.'

'In the end I did get something, but it didn't amount to much. Between them this knockabout couple thought that they did remember a red sports car paying for admission. Fred (or maybe it was Harry) had an idea that it was carrying a G.B. plate at the rear; and Harry (or possibly Fred) said it might have been on M.G.'

'An M.G. with a G.B. plate —'

'They're only possibilities, sir. We should have a right old pantomime, I can tell you, if we got the Loakes brothers anywhere near the witness box. One of these barrister chaps would have the court in stitches in no time.'

'That's more than likely. Half the time we policemen are

fighting the lawyers as well as the villains. Still, don't run yourself down, lad – an M.G. with G.B. plates, it might help.'

'In a way it does —'

'Don't tell me you've found out something more. What are you after? My job?'

Young Foster grinned. 'Not yet, sir. Yes, I did find a bit more. I don't know if you remember the Rectory Field: the one where they have the gymkhana —'

'I've seen it, of course.'

'All the cars coming away from it have to use the one track to get to the road and when they reach the road they must turn either left or right.

'If they are coming into Amminster they turn right; and if they are heading out into the country they turn left.

'Now we know that the red sports car turned right because when the chap who was driving it called out "Hallo Barbara", or whatever it was he said, he was actually overtaking Mrs Benson with her little group who were walking back into the town to catch their bus.

'Gymkhana day is a bit of an annual turn-out for Amminster. When all the cars start coming away from it quite a lot of people along High Parade stand about to watch them. So someone might have noticed a red M.G. and the people in it. Or of course the car might have called at Wilson's Garage for petrol. I didn't think it was a big chance, but it was an idea —'

'It was a damned good idea, too, lad. Did you have any luck with it?'

'Up to a point; yes. Spider Stokes was on the petrol pumps in the forecourt of the garage and of course he notices cars; he's car mad. Open sports cars aren't all that common these days and he spotted the M.G. because of that. But there was another reason to. The car stopped halfway along High Parade outside Williams, the newsagent and tobacconist.

162

'Spider saw a chap jump out and go into the shop and come out again in a couple of minutes presumably with a packet of fags. Just as he was getting back into the car Williams darted out after him and handed him something.

'Spider didn't really think anything of it; but standing there waiting for the next customer to drive up to the pumps he noticed it and when I came along asking questions of course he remembered it all.'

'Presumably you called on Williams next?'

'Right away, sir. Williams remembered the incident perfectly well. *He'd* be all right if ever we had to put him in the witness box.'

'What had he got to say?'

'This good-looking young gentleman, that's how he described him, this good-looking young gentleman came in and asked for West End cigarettes. Well, of course, not everybody stocks West Ends, they're what you might call a class smoke, hand-made; but as it happens Williams does keep them and the chap was delighted.

'He pulled out a pound note to pay for a packet of twenty, then he spotted a box of a hundred at the back and decided to take that.

'A quid wouldn't pay for a hundred, of course, so he then got a fiver out of his note-case.

'He was in a hurry because the car was stopped on a double yellow line and one way and another there was a muddle over the money. Williams had already started to give change for the first pound note, then the fiver was produced and finally when the chap went out of the shop with the box of a hundred he left the original pound note behind on the counter.

'Williams spotted it; ran out with it; and was just in time to catch the chap before he drove off again.

'So naturally he remembered the episode and incidentally he had a jolly good look at the man in the M.G.

'I've got a good description of him, sir, in my notebook

163

rather better than the "average height, medium colour" sort of stuff; and what's more Williams is quite sure he would recognise a photograph of this chap if he saw one.'

'We must get him up here right away then to look through our picture gallery,' the inspector said. 'You never know; we might be lucky.'

'That's what I thought, sir.'

'You've done well, Foster. Keep plugging away at it. Organise Williams and the rogues gallery and let me know at once if you get any developments.'

'Of course, sir.'

After the young detective had left his office the inspector sat for a while at his desk; not reading; not writing; staring rather vacantly at the blank wall opposite, thinking.

He had said, 'You've done well, Foster,' and he meant it. Young Foster had done well. Nobody knew better than William Lawson that it was nearly always a succession of innumerable questions which eventually led to the first real clue in any case. He would energetically support any local inquiries about the red M.G. with a G.B. plate and a good-looking young driver who smoked West End hand-made cigarettes; but the inspector was too old a hand to ignore his instincts; and when he gazed across his office and tried to make his mind as blank as the wall at which he was staring his instinct said a single word to him. And that word was neither 'Amminster' nor 'Gymkhana'; it was 'Tooveys'.

XVI

We've got to help ourselves; we've got to do something, Barbara had said. Her words hadn't produced any noticeable reaction from Vyvyan at the time, and for the next few days they set the tone of bitter discussion and recrimination between them.

In this bitter wrangling the woman dominated. *If two people sit on a horse one must ride behind,* a supremely commonsensical Englishman said a long time ago, and it was now tacitly recognised between these two who rode behind and who was in the saddle.

To Barbara's disgust Vyvyan seemed to be content with fatalistic apathy.

'If only you would stop drinking that damned stuff long enough to listen,' she said angrily.

Vyvyan poured himself out another whisky.

'I could hear you if I was dead drunk, you're making such a noise about all this.'

'And you're content to sit back and do nothing? Lie down and let Peter Venning walk all over us? Christ, Vyvyan, I thought you had more guts.'

The man flushed slightly.

'It's not a question of guts. It's a question of common sense.'

'That's what they all say when they turn tail and run, isn't it?'

'The best thing we can do is to give Venning the five thousand he wants to keep his mouth shut.'

'I don't believe it ever pays to give in to blackmail – everybody says that.'

'For God's sake be your age. What position are we in to

165

do anything about it? First of all we've got to get actual proof that he is blackmailing us, that he is threatening us; *if you don't hand over five thousand I'll get you put away* —'

'We could probably trap him into that. Make him come here for the money and have a tape-recorder going.'

'So then we go to the police and say look, we lifted twenty-seven thousand pounds out of Barrolds bank at Amminster and we are having trouble about splitting it up. We should have trouble right enough then. Seven years trouble most likely. *Seven years!*'

'What do you suggest we do, then?'

'What *can* we do? Venning has only got to go to the police and say he remembers whom he sold that gun to; they bring Mrs Benson here to identify you and the thing is busted wide open.'

'You're content to give in, go quietly?'

Vyvyan drained his glass and set it down. He was now slightly muzzy with the amount of drink he had taken. Barbara watching him with cold, hard eyes, despised him for his stupid inert muzziness.

'I accept the fact that I've been a b.f.,' he said. 'That evening, in St John's Wood, talking to those two chaps it all seemed a good idea; this perfect crime business; I started to talk about it just for the sake of an argument, to say something different from what they were saying. Then I got hooked on to the idea. And then – well, you know the rest. If something goes wrong the only sensible thing to do is to realise that it has gone wrong; cut your losses; accept the fact . . .'

His words died away inconclusively and after a few seconds' silence Barbara said, '*I* don't accept it. I don't accept that we've got to do whatever Peter Venning says. I don't accept that we can't do anything about it.'

When the telephone bell sounded half an hour later Vyvyan didn't attempt to answer it. He wasn't interested in who it was and he was content that Barbara should deal with it.

As she moved towards the instrument she somehow knew that she would hear Venning's voice at the other end.

It was Venning's voice, right enough; as smooth, oily and dangerous as ever.

'It's about a week since we had our little chat,' Venning said, 'and I did say a week, didn't I?'

'What's all that supposed to mean?'

'It means, my dear Barbara, that I should like to see you here at the shop, tomorrow.'

Barbara hesitated a moment; then tried to temporise with, 'It would suit us better if you come here.'

Venning was amused. 'I'm sure it would. But this is a question of what suits *me*, my dear. What suits *me*. I'm afraid you must accustom yourself to that idea. What suits *me*. And it suits me for you to come here. There won't be any nonsense about tape-recorders, or anything like that then, will there? Tomorrow.'

Barbara was silent so that after a few seconds his voice came again.

'Tomorrow. You heard me all right, did you, Barbara?'

'Yes, I heard you.'

'At seven. No, say seven-thirty. And you know what to bring with you. O.K.?'

'O.K.' Barbara forced herself to make the reply, but as she put down the receiver her hand was shaking and her face white with anger.

When she came back from the telephone recess into the living-room she said, 'That was Venning.'

Vyvyan who had begun to watch TV asked almost absently, 'Venning? What did he want?'

The casualness of his tone infuriated Barbara even further.

'Want? Oh nothing much. He was just giving me orders about what I've got to do and when I've got to do it. He says it will suit him if I go round to the shop tomorrow at

167

half past seven with the five thousand pounds he's asking for. That's all he wants.'

Vyvyan was silent for a few moments as though he were giving the problem serious thought; but ultimately all he said was, 'Well, you had better do it then and get it over, hadn't you?'

Barbara was bitterly angry. 'I wonder you don't ask me to take a bunch of flowers round to the bastard,' she said.

Vyvyan might not have heard her. He continued to look at the inanities on the television screen . . .

The following day was an unhappy one for Vyvyan. The temporary, and well-paid post which he had been lucky enough to step into immediately after walking out of T.M. & F. had come to an end. For a few days nothing happened; the expected chopper didn't fall and Vyvyan began to fool himself that it wasn't going to fall . . . he must have done so well in the temporary job, he told himself, that they were going to offer to keep him on permanently . . .

This was the hope he carried with him when, the day after his worst row with Barbara, he was summoned by the two directors into their office. It was true that the possibility of keeping him on for an extended term had been discussed between them; but it was a short discussion only, terminated by the younger of the two men raising his right forearm and elbow suggestively . . .

Shortly before six Vyvyan walked into the Bombardier. His normal time for coming in was midday so that Mrs Bennett was mildly surprised to see him.

The only other occupant of the bar was the little man whom Vyvyan remembered as 'the rat peering out of a lavatory brush'; who was as mad as a coot and who talked about astrology.

'Have a glass of Madeira,' Vyvyan invited him.

'I don't mind if I do, sir. Delighted in fact. But how did you know I drink Madeira wine?'

'I remember you from last time.'

'Ah – and I remember you now, sir. A Leo, aren't you? A critical year for us Leos, sir. I'm sure of it. Money-wise I mean. I hope things are going well for you.'

Vyvyan accepted his customary large Scotch from Mrs Bennett and considered his reply. Eventually he said, 'My father died earlier in the year and he was a pretty rich man.'

'Ah well, there you are, sir. Out of sorrow shall come strength as the good book says.'

'Not all that much actually. He left me precisely two hundred and fifty pounds.'

'If he had left you a fortune, Mr Weighman,' (Mrs Bennett habitually addressed him by name these days, an accolade which she bestowed on scarcely anybody else) 'if he had left you a fortune you would probably have done something silly with it.'

Vyvyan gave a short harsh laugh. 'I've done something silly without it.'

'We all do silly things, don't we?'

He considered her. Difficult to think of that paragon ever doing anything silly – certainly nothing so silly as imagining she could commit a perfect crime and then laying herself open to blackmail from her partner's former employer.

'What have you done silly, Mrs B?' (this was the utmost familiarity he could bring himself to use with her; 'Ethel' he simply could not achieve).

She smiled. 'No good thinking back on them now, is it?'

'None at all.'

'There's always tomorrow.'

Vyvyan pushed his glass forward for replenishment and said, 'There are times when I think that's just about the most depressing statement anyone can make.'

When Vyvyan finally made a slightly unsteady exit from the Bombardier the rat-behind-the-lavatory-brush, still with a half-finished glass of Madeira in front of him, said, 'Your friend has got a nimbus on him.'

'A nimbus?' Mrs Bennett wasn't sure what a nimbus was.

'Round his head. A cloudy thing. Something there. Misty. An atmosphere. It's bad.'

'Bad?'

'*His* is. I don't say it's death, but it's *bad*. It's wrong. It's a disaster nimbus.'

'You mean he's going to have an accident?'

'Could be. Something of the sort. When Leos go wrong they go wrong badly as a rule. I'd say he's made a mess of things, that one.'

'So many men do,' Mrs Bennett said and picked up a glass to polish it.

On her way back to Hambledon Street Barbara walked along the crowded pavement of the King's Road without really seeing the familiarly odd assortment of humanity that jostled there. She had plenty to occupy her thoughts, her bitter, angry, frustrated, revenge-seeking thoughts . . .

. . . so that was what blackmail was like . . . painless in a way . . . it didn't seem to mean anything . . . a bundle of paper notes . . . the bastard didn't even count them . . . just took them and smiled, '*You're a sensible girl, Barbara, I'm sure you haven't tried anything funny*' . . . sensible! So sensible I've got myself – I've let somebody else get me – into a jam where I can be made to jump through the hoop as often as he likes . . .

Somehow there had been an air of unreality about the whole thing. Venning hadn't even been unpleasant . . . why should the bastard be unpleasant when he was picking up five thousand pounds . . . *I miss you in the shop, Barbara; in spite of our little differences we always got on quite well together* . . . *sensible girl* . . . *no hard feelings on either side I'm sure* . . . *good-bye* . . .

Barbara let herself into the flat. Whether Vyvyan would be there or not she didn't know; their movements and engagements were not much discussed with one another these days.

But he was in, sprawled in the one large armchair.

Either asleep or drunk. In all probability both if he was running true to form.

The sight of him – the face coarser than it used to be, the mouth sagging open, the whole posture ungainly – revolted her. Revolted and infuriated ... *men* she thought. They use you, batten on you, betray you, squeeze money out of you ... they didn't amount to much really; in the long run you had to look after yourself ... *give me the knife* ... standing there in the small, quiet comfortable living-room of the Hambledon Street flat, looking down on the inert form of the man she now despised, the thought came to her, *if one perfect crime, why not another?*

XVII

'Couldn't you possibly come down to the cottage for the week-end?' Stella Margerrison asked.

Barbara said she would probably be able to manage it.

'You angel! I can't think how I got landed with this Caley-Dawson couple. It's a family thing. Too complicated to explain. And boring anyway. He really is the true Poonah-ite. I expect he'll be disappointed not to find punkah-wallahs in the cottage. It will be too wonderful if you can be there to lighten the atmosphere a bit; and there will be a gay young man, anyway. Willie Tremuller, you know the one whose father has just got into the Cabinet.'

Barbara nodded. She was well enough up in the social gossip of the town to know young Willie Tremuller by name.

'And you're sure you don't mind coming by yourself?' Stella queried.

'Rather a relief, really.'

'That Vyvyan of yours is proving difficult, is he?'

'I can handle him.'

Stella was quick to notice the touch of grimness in the words. She approved of it. Underneath her deceptively fluffy exterior she was a dedicated feminist.

'You're quite tough really, aren't you, Bar?' she said.

'It seems to me women have to be tough to survive,' Barbara answered, 'and I don't see any point in not surviv-ing' . . .

On their way out of London Stella, who drove well and fast, said, 'We have to stick to the A23 for about thirty miles but once we leave it we get into really rustic parts.'

So indeed it turned out.

Names like Nightingale Corner, Ramsbottom Lane and Parson's Pleasure showed up on the signposts; roads narrowed into lanes; lanes deepened almost into ravines between high green banks reminiscent more of the West Country than of Sussex.

There were some small pinkwashed houses round a pond; some thatched roofs among green trees; an inn with a swinging sign: The Cricketers; and, turning sharply into a drive on the left-hand side Stella said, 'Here we are. Back of beyond land. Gorse Bank Cottage.'

The cottage in essence was old and simple. Half timbered; wattle and daub; thatch; low ceilings; small windows. Outside it still looked much as it had done through its four hundred years; inside dreadful liberties had been taken with its character and dignity to meet an effete generation's obsession with warmth and comfort.

Barbara thoroughly approved of them all.

'What a divine little place,' she exclaimed.

'It's rather sweet, isn't it? I'll go and see where everybody is and get Willie to fix the drinks and then we'll all meet before dinner.'

The evening wasn't anything like as bad as Stella, on the way down, had warned Barbara it might be.

Colonel Caley-Dawson – thin; yellowy-brown in complexion; aged probably an old sixty-five but quite possibly a young eighty-five; with small eyes of an extraordinary blueness, could obviously be described – in fact he so described himself – as a stick-in-the-mud.

But it had to be admitted that the mud the colonel chose to stick in was not without its interesting qualities.

One of his manias was for eating dried grass. But as he explained it – *natural food; plenty of it; no starvation; the cow eats grass, we eat the cow, why not short cut? delicious taste* – it didn't sound like a mania at all, it sounded like rather amusing common sense.

After dinner Stella switched on the TV and its inanities

seemed singularly, almost indecently, inappropriate in that remote rusticity.

The grass-eating colonel, after viewing it for some minutes, said succinctly, 'Shepherd singing ragtime.'

Which somehow seemed such a neat and devastating summary that Stella leant forward and turned the machine off. Shortly afterwards everybody went to bed.

Next day Stella Margerrison's first announcement was, 'I'm going to be kitchen-bound for a while so you must all amuse yourselves.'

At the back of the cottage there was a croquet-lawn to which the Caley-Dawsons hastened with the shining light of fanaticism in their eyes.

'Don't get caught up in that,' was Willie Tremuller's whispered advice to Barbara. 'Let's go and explore.'

Willie was a tall young man with a large head, physically unimpressive but conversationally stimulating.

Barbara found him amusing company and he quite evidently thought the same about her.

'Let's explore,' meant getting into Willie's Triumph and, as he put it, 'whirling round the lanes.'

It was something to do, and Willie's dryly amusing conversation made it good fun.

As Willie himself said, 'There isn't really much point in it. But Stella obviously wants us out of the way, and when we get back we shall feel, quite unjustifiably of course, that we have done something to earn her marvellous pre-lunch drinks.'

It was an unknown part of the world to Barbara and the last thing she expected to see was a signpost in the hedge-row pointing up a side turning and bearing the three words *Mill Race House*.

She had, as it happened, been thinking about Peter Venning at that moment, which was hardly strange seeing that since her last interview with the man in Tooveys he had seldom been absent from her thoughts.

'*Mill Race House!*' she exclaimed; they were thirty yards past the signpost now and Willie applied the brakes.

'Do you know it?'

'I'd like to have a look at it.'

'What is it? A stately mansion?'

'No, nothing like that. Somebody I know either has bought it or is thinking of buying it.'

'Let's take a dekko,' Willie said amiably.

The acute turning into the side road, itself situated at a dangerous bend, excited humorous comments from Willie about the lethal illogicality of English roads generally.

The short narrow side road turned out to be not so much a road as a drive, because it didn't apparently go beyond the Mill House.

'For Sale' a large red and white notice announced; and across this a small sticker had been pasted diagonally: 'SOLD.'

'Your chum has bought the place apparently,' Willie said.

'Not so much a chum as a business acquaintance.'

'Well, he knows an attractive place when he sees one.'

The Mill House was undoubtedly, attractive.

It was a square, well-proportioned house built actually across the mill race which could be heard noisily hurrying along.

When they started to walk round the house and its outbuildings it was obvious that everything had been neglected for some time.

'Your, what was it you called him, business acquaintance?, will have to spend a bit of money on the outfit,' Willie said.

'After five thousand pounds, he reckons.'

'He'll probably find he'll want more than that.'

'Quite possibly,' Barbara said dryly.

She could see the possibilities of the place for selling antiques. Supervising its conversion into a dwelling-house and showroom would, in fact, be just the sort of job she

175

would enjoy.

'It's a spooky sort of place,' Willie said as they walked round. 'Are you psychic? Do you feel things?'

'Not in the slightest,' Barbara laughed, adding as a quick afterthought. 'Anger, of course, occasionally. What's spooky about it, anyway?'

At that moment they were on a rickety bridge connecting a store shed with the Mill House itself. Six feet below them the water of the race foamed and thundered along.

The wooden hand-rail looked so untrustworthy that Willie wisely refrained from leaning on it.

'What a place for a murder,' he said. 'Push anyone over here and he'd be swept under the paddles of the wheel in no time and wouldn't stand a chance. No wonder it feels spooky. I expect half a dozen millers have got rid of their troublesome wives here; or the other way round, of course.'

'You've got a morbid imagination, Willie,' Barbara said. 'Splendidly morbid.'

Venning was busy dealing with one of his richest and trickiest customers when the door opened and a quick glance showed him that Barbara had come into the shop.

He was surprised, but he couldn't afford to speculate about the matter until the negotiations with Mrs Wartenburg (now in a delicate stage) were completed.

Once again he drew her attention to the two silver sauce-boats.

'They really are most beautiful Georgian work,' he said temptingly.

'If it wasn't beautiful I shouldn't want it,' Mrs Wartenburg snapped.

The trouble between them lay in the fact that mainly for reasons of eccentricity the rich, fat, overfed, under-exercised old woman from South Kensington wanted to buy one sauce boat only and to 'think about' the other one.

Venning repeated his objection to this. 'They are so ob-

176

viously a pair. I'm sure that with your knowledge of these things you can't really expect me to split them up.'

'At the price you are asking I don't know that I can afford to buy both of them.'

'Mrs Wartenburg, when you can't afford the extremely modest figure' (*at least three times what he paid for it*, thought Barbara who was following these exchanges with sardonic interest) 'the *extremely* modest figure I have put on this pair of sauce boats, then' – Venning raised his hands in mock horror at such a suggestion – 'things will be bad indeed.'

The fleshy face creased into a grimace. 'They're pretty bad now. But, still, all right – I suppose they *are* a pair after all. I'll take the two of them. But don't expect me in here again for a long time, Mr Venning.'

'My dear lady you are always welcome whenever you want to come. Just to look round and amuse yourself.'

'An expensive amusement,' Mrs Wartenburg said, getting out her cheque book with stubby and be-ringed fingers.

Success in selling the two Georgian sauce boats put Venning in a good humour and when the door finally closed behind Mrs Wartenburg it was with something approaching an amiable curiosity that he turned to Barbara.

'A nice little sale,' he said.

'If that old trout paid ten times what I asked her she simply wouldn't know the money had gone out of her account. She's loaded with it.'

'It's more or less shutting up time, isn't it?'

... she wants to talk, Venning thought; *now, what about?* He was intrigued. Barbara had always possessed this double pull over him: infuriating him by her superiority, yet interesting him by her personality.

He crossed to the door; locked it; put the 'Closed' notice in position and said, 'Let's sit in the office and be comfortable.'

They settled in chairs on either side of the minute gas-fire, Venning's brain meanwhile working overtime.

... the word *trap* had immediately come into his mind; but the more he thought about it the less likely it seemed ... if he had been invited to Hambledon Street, if this meeting had been taking place there, in Weighman's flat, then *trap* would be a high possibility with the chances of bugging the room before he came, or even of hiding a detective behind a curtain ... but here, in his own office? ... and in any case it wasn't possible for them even to threaten him without cutting their own throats ... so what? ...

He was more intrigued than ever; but if there were any cards to be put on the table he was determined that Barbara's should go down first.

'Well,' he said, 'here we are. You've called round to see me, and the shop door is shut. Presumably you want to say something —'

She smiled at him, 'Yes, I do, Peter —' *will you come into my parlour* was jingling in her head again, but which now was spider, which fly, she thought ...

'Yes, I do, Peter. I've been thinking over what you were telling me about having to move away from here. Even with selling Georgian silver sauce boats to rich old ladies you can't pay an extra three thousand a year rent, I do see that.'

'Mrs Wartenburg doesn't come in every day, anyway.'

'Where's this place you said you were thinking of going to?'

Venning was still wary ... I wonder what this one is up to, he thought ... a bad enemy she would make, but a good ally ... he had already told her the name of the place, no harm in repeating it ...

'Mill Race House.'

'And where is it?'

'Sussex. Out in the wilds.'

'And will you have to spend a lot on it?'

'Quite a lot. I've already got something towards that. Five thousand pounds. Or had you forgotten?'

178

'No. I haven't forgotten, Peter. That's why I'm here.'

'I thought it might be. But I don't quite see how.'

'Is five thousand going to be enough?'

Venning stared at her. He didn't quite know what to make of this. He would have to be cautious, of course; but he felt comfortably confident that he held all the aces.

At length he said, 'I could always ask for more.'

'That's exactly what I have been thinking.'

'Just what *have* you been thinking, Barbara?'

'Well, for one thing I've been thinking over what you said at our last meeting. You said that we always got on well when I was working here and that you missed me—'

Venning laughed. 'Difficult for you to believe, of course, I can see that. But actually it's true. I didn't like the damned superior airs you sometimes gave yourself; but apart from that, yes I *do* miss you.'

Barbara let the 'damned superior airs' taunt go by. It wasn't in her present strategy to quarrel.

'I miss coming here,' she said. 'I enjoyed it.'

'So what?'

'And you also said, if you remember, about this place that you've discovered in Sussex, or wherever it is, "You must come down and have a look at it and tell me what to do." '

'Is that what you are proposing?'

Barbara leant forward.

'I don't know if things have altered here, but in that small compartment under those shelves there always used to be a bottle, two glasses and a siphon of soda —'

Silently Venning bent down; opened the cubby-hole; drew out a bottle of Glenfiddich, two glasses and the siphon; poured out two generous drinks; splashed soda into his own and invited Barbara to do the same for herself.

'So what do we drink to?' he asked; he was becoming interested.

179

'What would you say to a partner, *a partner*, who can be of genuine help in the business and who could bring, oh I don't know, quite a lot of money into it straight away?'

He didn't say anything, just continued to look at her with those fishy eyes, speculatively. But she felt certain that things were going the way she wanted them to ...

Again she leant forward, confidentially.

'Look, Peter, this isn't easy for me. If you want to be a bastard about it and turn me down flat, say so; and I'll walk out.'

'Who said anything about turning you down? I'm interested.'

'All right then, I'm washed up with Vyvyan Weighman. I've been a fool about him.'

'I don't suppose you've been the only one.'

'Perhaps not. I'm not interested in all that, in a way. It's what he did to me, what I let him do to me, that's where I was a fool. He talked me into this business at Amminster; a lot of hooey about planning the perfect crime; I never wanted to do it; but I did it, so I can't complain; it was my own fault. Now the result is that I'm tied up with an alcoholic who's drinking all the money away. I want to use it before it's all gone.'

'So what's the proposition?'

'I want to go down with you to this house you've found in Sussex and see what it looks like. I'm sure it's all right, or you wouldn't have chosen it, but there may be things I can advise in, like alterations and decorating and so on. Then I want to pick up what's left of the Amminster money, and bring it into the business as your partner. Vyvyan can go on drinking himself silly in the Bombardier or wherever it is he goes all the time.'

After a considerable pause Venning broke into what for him was a broad smile.

'I didn't think you had so much sense, Barbara,' he said.

180

'I'm going down to Sussex on Wednesday. You can meet me there if you like.'

'Let's drink to that, then,' said the Spider, raising her glass, now very well content with the evening's work.

XVIII

On Tuesday evening Barbara said, 'I shall want the car to-morrow. I'm going down to Stella Margerrison's cottage in Sussex.'

'I was at prep School in Sussex. Near Haywards Heath. Is she anywhere in that direction?'

'Not really.'

'I might come down with you and have a potter round while you're doing your business with her.'

As Barbara had no intention of visiting Gorse Bank Cottage and certainly didn't want Vyvyan with her on her trip this tentative suggestion had to be firmly quashed before it grew into anything.

Barbara quashed it.

Her 'that wouldn't do at all. Stella doesn't want two of us, and anyway you would simply be in and out of all the local pubs all day getting stupidly tight. I'll go alone,' was brusque enough in all conscience.

Just for a moment she thought he might show some of his old spirit and fly back at her, telling her in no uncertain manner where she got off and just exactly what the hell she could do with her dictatorial manners.

She almost wanted him to.

But Vyvyan merely looked slightly sheepish and busied himself mixing another drink. These days he accepted whatever directions she chose to give, merely shrugging mental shoulders and telling himself that it was less trouble that way and that the true philosophy of life lay in saying *what the hell* and not troubling.

The woman wasn't really surprised at his reaction, or lack of it. When she had first come to live with Vyvyan

182

there had been an edge on things; she had even been slightly scared of the dark mood he could show at times. Looking back she thought that perhaps it had been the being scared, the occasional sense of fear, that had supplied the edge to living; just as now it was the feeling of power that gave a zest to things and made her feel good.

Nowadays Vyvyan did what she told him. It was the other man, Venning, she had to fear. As long as he was about he had the whip hand over her; he barked out the orders and she had to jump through the hoop. Venning meant danger; and to Barbara Courlander danger didn't mean shutting one's eyes and piously hoping the nasty thing would go away (as, apparently it now did to Vyvyan); it meant a challenge; and a challenge in her book meant a fight; and in a fight one side won and the other lost . . .

She didn't know what her relations with Vyvyan would be when Peter Venning was out of the way; she was conscious that there was still a bond between them. Physical pleasure which was still hungry and almost savage in its execution . . . But Venning wasn't yet out of the way; so she repeated her intentions to Vyvyan, 'I shall want the Volvo tomorrow for most of the day, so don't you plan to do anything with it.'

To Stella Margerrison, of course, she had to tell a different tale. It was with some diffidence that she had said she wanted to take a day off since the shop in Curzon Terrace was doing good business and there was normally quite enough work there to keep them both occupied.

But there is one line of approach from one woman to another which is never used in vain.

'Stella, I know it's a frightful bore, but tomorrow I do want to have a day off in the country for – well, you know, a *particular reason*—'

'Charles?'

Barbara smiled and said nothing. Which in Stella Margerrison's book was all according to the rules of the game. She hadn't really expected that Barbara would say anything too specific.

'My dear, how exciting!'

Barbara made a slight gesture with her hands, the sort of gesture which might have meant, *I don't have to tell you a thing about all this; it's woman to woman stuff and you can guess it all; and I know you won't breathe a word about it to anybody* . . .

'He's rather a dear, isn't he?' Stella said.

'Charles is sweet.'

'*Of course* you must be off for the day. My dear, we shall be calling you *your Grace* before we know where we are, I can see that.'

The memory of this conversation, and thoughts branching from it, kept Barbara amused most of the way down to the hinterland of Sussex . . . it was fun fooling people to the top of their bent, fun seeing just how much you could get away with . . . if you were skilful enough; careful enough; chose just the right words moment, actions, people believed you . . . *nothing need go wrong* . . . Vyvyan had said that and Vyvyan had been right . . . how did it go in Shakespeare? *but screw your courage to the sticking point and we'll not fail* . . . correction: *I* not we; I'll not fail; *give me the knife* . . .

Mill Race House was so hidden away that she had some difficulty in finding it again; but eventually she came upon the dangerous bend in the road, which she recognised, and there was the signpost MILL RACE HOUSE.

She negotiated the sharp turn into the rutted track and drove slowly up to the house.

Venning had an appointment with the Vendor's solicitors in the nearby town and had told her if he wasn't there when she arrived to wait for him.

No question of, 'I may be slightly late so you mustn't mind hanging on for a bit'; just a brutally blunt 'if I'm not there when you arrive, wait'.

184

The order and the peremptory tone in which it was given were not lost on Barbara, but she accepted them. She knew the shallows of Venning's mind pretty well by now; if he was going to accept her he was going to make it very plain on what terms that acceptance would be – *his* terms ... *thank God he won't want to start any bed business*, she thought, *I really don't think I could stomach that with him* ...

She began a slow methodical tour of inspection of the whole premises, the Mill House itself and the various outbuildings, some of them well-built stone affairs, some not much more than sheds that had grown up around it.

As she went round she was conscious of the fact that her mind was operating on two levels; and she found that she could be sufficiently objective to be amused by her own powers of double thinking.

On one level she was genuinely interested in the possibilities of the place as an antique showroom and shop. The house had character and charm; she could see that restoring it would be interesting and rewarding.

There was no doubt that it could be made very attractive. Apart from the house itself various things were crying out to be done: a good wrought-iron sign in the roadway, she thought, something sufficiently well-made to set the tone for the entire place and the quality of goods to be found in it; then the drive would certainly have to be improved, *not* turned into an impeccably smooth piece of tarmac of course, but given at least a reasonable surface; and the terribly neglected grounds which in their present state hardly justified the description 'garden', something surely could be made of them...

And all these things – dwelling-house, outbuildings and grounds – were centred on one thing, and in a way subservient to it – the tinkling, hurrying, noisy race of water that ran so swiftly and so dangerously beneath the small bridge with the flimsy hand-rail ...

While Barbara was standing on the bridge, one hand resting lightly on the rail, Venning drove up from the road and brought his car to a halt beside the Volvo.

She was a good driver herself and she wasn't much impressed by the way Venning handled his car ... maybe he wasn't so hot at other things either, she thought, maybe Peter Venning wasn't quite as clever as he imagined himself to be ...

He was considerably late, but he didn't apologise for the fact. His interview with the solicitors had been full of frustrating snags and queries and he was in a bad temper.

'I'm glad you had the sense to come,' was his first greeting.

Barbara knew that he wanted to provoke her and she didn't intend to let herself be provoked. Her grip tightened ever so slightly on that satisfyingly insecure rail and she smiled.

'I wanted to come.'

He was slightly mollified by her amiability.

'Good. What do you think of it?'

'I think you're on to a good thing here, Peter.'

'You think I can make something of it?'

'I'm sure you can.'

'Let's take a walk round.'

Together they went slowly over the same ground which Barbara had covered by herself.

As they went Venning outlined his own ideas for the conversion and adaptation of the various parts of the building. Most of the ideas Barbara thought were good; when she ventured to differ from him and to suggest some alternative he did not fail to snub her rudely; as far as he was concerned Barbara Courlander had come to an end of prancing on her high horse. She knew it; and he knew it; and it was an agreeable feeling.

But, deliberately rude though he allowed himself to be, he knew well enough that when it came to suggestions about the interior decorating and furnishing of the place she could be of real help to him. She had a flair in these things and he proposed to use that flair.

Eventually they finished their tour of inspection and were back again on the little bridge which, standing as it did between the main store shed and the Mill House itself, was a sort of focal point of the whole property.

'Well,' he repeated his question. 'What do you think of it?

'I think you've been extremely clever to find it, Peter.'

He didn't find the flattery unpleasant.

'Of course it's a bit out of the way,' he said.

'We could have a map printed on the back of our card showing where the place is and how to get here. I know a man who would do it splendidly, and give us something attractive and amusing.'

'I wouldn't lean too heavily against that rail,' Venning said. 'It doesn't look any too safe to me.'

Barbara laughed easily, 'Oh, it's O.K.,' she said.

'O.K. for you maybe,' Venning took her up sourly. 'You fall in if you want to. You can probably swim like a fish. I can't swim a yard and I don't propose to start learning here.'

If Barbara took in what he said she gave no sign of having done so.

'Of course this stream really *makes* the place,' she said.

'Damned noisy all the time.'

'It's a splendid noise, Peter. Anybody living here would get so used to it they wouldn't hear it after the first week; and people coming to look round and buy would be enchanted by it.'

Venning thought that was probably true. 'Maybe,' he allowed himself to agree, and then added, 'You can start the wheel going if you want to. It still works.'

'It does? How marvellous. How do you start it?'

Immediately inside the Mill House was a ponderous wooden lever. With some difficulty Venning moved it through ninety degrees into a new position and when they both stepped outside on to the bridge again the huge cumbersome wheel was already beginning to revolve.

Barbara watched it gathering speed in fascination . . .

Venning went into the house and pushed the lever back into the 'off' position.

When he came outside again he said, 'I expect you've realised one thing —'

For a moment Barbara was disconcerted by the remark; but she consoled herself with the thought that he wasn't a mind-reader and she was relieved when he went on : '— Five thousand pounds isn't going all that far here.'

'How much are you giving for the place?'

'I don't know that it's got anything to do with you.'

'Oh, come off it for God's sake, Peter. Of course it's got something to do with me. If we are going to be partners, let's be partners.'

After a moment's reflection he nodded and said, 'Twelve thousand five hundred. And it's more than I've got.'

'I've told you about the Amminster money.'

Tell me about Amminster itself. Doing the job. I mean. What was it like? That au pair business —?'

'On the whole that was rather a bore.'

'I can't see you as the perfect au pair, I must say.'

'There was riding with the children, that wasn't too bad.'

'And actually holding-up the bank manager – what was that like?'

Barbara shugged her shoulders. 'Oh, I don't know . . . I've forgotten . . .' But, of course, she hadn't forgotten. She remembered it all vividly. She remembered the moment of pressing the dummy gun against the back of Benson's skull; she remembered the terror which had petrified the little man and had communicated itself so pleasurably to her; she remembered saying, and enjoying saying, *this is a gun. Don't shout or try anything funny, or I'll blow your head off*; she remembered subsequently telling Vyvyan the sensation she had got out of it ... *like being in bed with you* ... all this she remembered vividly as she looked at Peter Venning standing with his back to the flimsy guard rail of the bridge and all the time the mill race thundering below ...

He moved suddenly.

'Too noisy here,' he said. 'Let's move away a bit.'

They walked as far as the two cars in the drive and leaning against his Venning resumed the conversation, 'All right. Money. If we are going to be partners, let's talk about the money. The papers said you got twenty-seven thousand out of the bank at Amminster. Is that right?'

'Near enough.'

'So what have you got now?'

'Just over twenty thousand, I suppose. You've had five and we've spent a little. Something over twenty.'

'In that flat of yours?'

'Where else can we keep it?'

'In notes?'

'Of course it's in notes.'

'Fantastic. I wish I had twenty thousand stacked away in notes here.'

'You can have. I'll bring it down here to you.'

Venning studied her carefully. He realised that he had the whip hand over her, but even so —

'What else is there for me to do?' she broke into his thoughts. 'It's no good trying to go on with Vyvyan. And I don't want to try, anyway. Like I told you Vyvyan and I are washed up absolutely. It will take him some time to drink his way through that amount of cash, but by God he's doing his best; and it's no fun for me being there while he's doing it and having the money there is a nightmare, anyway.'

'Where is it? In a safe?'

'We haven't got a safe.'

'You mean it isn't locked away?'

'We haven't got a safe,' Barbara repeated.

'And what about Weighman?'

'What about him?'

'What's he going to do when he finds you gone and the money with you?'

'What can he do that won't land him in prison?'

Venning considered for a moment or two and finally said, 'Yes – but still —'

'I'll tell you the sensible thing to do with Vyvyan,' Barbara said.

'What's that?'

'Don't clear the money out absolutely completely. Leave two thousand behind. If we leave him nothing he might get so mad he'd do something silly, even if it meant spiting himself. In his present state two thousand pounds in notes will still look a lot of money, and he'll most likely be content to go on drinking it away as long as it lasts.'

Venning laughed. 'I should think that's a good piece of psychology.'

'Women are good psychologists – we have to be.'

Venning laughed again, not so pleasantly this time. 'Yes. Don't get too clever, though, will you? All right, I agree to that. Call it eighteen thousand; that's a nice round sum. Today week. Here, the same time as today. You bring the money down and we'll be in business together. O.K.?'

'That's what I want to do, Peter.'

'And Barbara —'

She looked at him inquiringly.

'– We'll be partners; but I'll be in charge of things. You be a sensible girl and do as I say and we'll get on fine. Start playing up in any way and there'll be trouble. Understood?'

... *Oh, you fat self-satisfied bastard,* Barbara thought, *you self-satisfied fat bastard* ...

She nodded submissively. 'Yes, Peter; quite understood.'

Barbara motored herself back to Hambledon Street, parked the Volvo half in the roadway, half on the pavement as usual and went into the flat.

Vyvyan wasn't in yet. Not that she expected him to be. If current form was anything to go by he would show up a great deal later, morose, taciturn, half pickled already and clearly intending to complete the job as the evening wore on.

At some point in the proceedings she would insist on being taken out to The Lobster Pot and, once there, if Vyvyan didn't feel inclined to eat anything that would be his look out; Barbara herself was excited and hungry and she proposed to order the best dinner which Gustave could provide . . .

She had a shower and changed into a comfortable trouser suit and was sitting watching the television when Vyvyan came in.

He sat down in the chair opposite her and said, 'Do we want this thing on?'

'Not particularly.' She switched it off.

Vyvyan looked white and ill; comparing him with the man she had known a year ago. Barbara suddenly felt shocked. Shocked and almost distressed.

'Have a drink,' she suggested, as she did so thinking it odd that the drinks which presumably he must have been having, probably ever since midday, didn't, for once, seem to be showing on him.

He shook his head and asked, 'How was your day in the country?'

'Oh, successful I think.'

'Successful?'

'Well, I mean I enjoyed it. Stella's always good fun.'

'Haywards Heath did you say?'

'Near there. Are you all right, Vyvyan?'

'All right? Yes; quite all right. Very much so, really.'

He didn't look all right; he looked ill.

Barbara got up and crossed to the drinks table, glass in hand. 'I'm having the other half,' she said. 'Shall I mix you one?'

'No, I don't think I'll have anything, thanks.'

It was clear that this astonishing statement would have to be given some elucidation sooner or later. For the moment Barbara let it pass.

When she sat down again opposite him, cradled her glass in her strong fingers and raised it to her lips for an obviously satisfying sip. Vyvyan said nothing but his hungry eyes followed every movement.

'I used to know round Haywards Heath,' he said.

'I know. You've told me all about that the other day. For God's sake, Vyvyan, I'm not dying to hear every scruffy detail of your prep-school days. Why won't you have a drink?'

'I'm thinking of giving it up.'

Barbara stared at him, assailed by a mixture of emotions – astonishment, incredulity, even amusement – which she found difficult to disentangle.

Eventually she asked, 'Have you been to a Harley Street man, or somebody, who told you you are drinking yourself to death? Is that it?'

'No, nothing to do with doctors. I don't think I should take much notice of anything they said anyway. No. Actually it was Mrs Bennett.'

... *Mrs Bennett* ... Barbara waited; but no more came. In one sense she wasn't surprised to hear another woman's name mentioned ... all in the game, of course ... in 1973, in S.W.3 love, if that's what you call it, was uninhibitedly free ... all the same she felt her claws instinctively unsheath themselves a little; her preserves might be tarnished slightly, faded from what they once were, but she didn't want anybody else trying to poach them ... all she could think of immediately was that if Mrs Bennett, whoever she was, made Vyvyan look as ill as he did at the moment she must be quite a woman ...

'And who the hell is Mrs Bennett?' she asked.

'She's at the Bombardier.'

'She's a barmaid there, do you mean?'

'Barmaid?' Vyvyan seemed to consider the word. 'Yes, I suppose you would call her that.'

'Well, what do you call her?'

The query made him laugh slightly.

'Actually I call her "Mrs B".'

'God, how twee.'

'Her Christian name is Ethel. I happen to know that. But of course, I've never called her by it.'

The oddest thing about that odd sentence seemed to Barbara to be the words 'of course'. She felt a strong desire to laugh.

'Are you telling me that you've been having an affair with some woman and you've never even used her Christian name yet?'

'Good God, I'm not having an affair with Mrs Bennett!' There was genuine shock in Vyvyan's voice. 'She's not that sort of woman.'

'I didn't know you recognised any other sort. What sort is this Mrs B of yours, then?'

'I would say she's an intensely religious woman,' Vyvyan answered, adding quickly, 'although, of course, I have never talked about religion with her.'

'What do you talk about with her?'

Vyvyan considered; hesitated; spoke at last.

'Nothing really. Nothing. It's just that she's – well, remarkable.'

Barbara looked at him for a second or two then, without speaking, went to the table where the drinks were and moving to one side so that he could follow her every action selected his favourite glass, filled it a third full of whisky, topped it up with soda, dropped in a piece of ice and brought it over to him.

She held it out.

'*My* prescription,' she said.

He hesitated.

'Go on. Drink it up. I don't like to see you taking too much of the stuff, but I don't like to see you in the state you are in this evening, either. Drink it up.'

Vyvyan stretched out a hand that shook a little and took the glass from her.

When he put it down, half empty, he said gratefully, 'You're quite right, I've been overdoing it. No sense in that, I know. I'll try to knock it off a bit.'

'Fair enough. It will be better fun all round if you do. Only for God's sake don't turn religious on me.

'No. It's just that I can't get out of my mind what a mess we're in. This fellow Venning. He's got us in a hopeless position. He can go on demanding anything he wants, and what can we do about it?'

Barbara said nothing.

'In a way I don't care,' Vyvyan went on. 'It's probably the best solution. Let him take the lot and then at least the thing is finished. In any case we can't stop him.'

'Oh, I don't know,' Barbara said. 'Something might happen.'

'What?'

'Heaven knows – he might fall down dead. People do . . .'

. . . looking back on Amminster one thing I am certain of is that Vyvyan was absolutely right in his ideas about the perfect crime. It can be done and it isn't too difficult to do. We had that silly little fusspot Benson exactly where we wanted him. It all worked perfectly. Then one of us, I don't believe it was me either, made the balls up about the gun . . . That's the only thing that went wrong . . . Well, no gun this time; no need for it; neater, my way; just a saw and an alibi. In all probability I shan't want the alibi but you never know. But I shall certainly want the saw . . . I'll ring Stella now, this minute . . . Stella, you don't have to tell me I'm being the most

frightful nuisance, but Charles, – well, you've no idea, the poor lamb really is getting wound up in a big way; he's got the loan of this cottage in the country, not all that far from you actually, Haywards Heath direction somewhere and he wants me to spend the day there with him . . . next Wednesday . . . talk about love in a cottage! But the point is I want a tale to satisfy Vyvyan, he's beginning to turn nasty about Charles . . . of course I can tell him to take a running jump at himself; maybe I will, too, before long; but I don't want to yet . . . if Vyvyan starts creating it will foul things up with Charles and he may take fright and disappear over the horizon and, let's face it, what girl wants to see a duke do that to her? I don't think anything is likely to crop up but Vyvyan may want to know what I'm doing with the car so, if any questions are asked, could you be a girl's best pal and swear blind I've been with you at the cottage all day . . .

So that was fixed. I'm going to spend the day with Stella in the country, I told Vyvyan, so I shall want the car. I don't know whether he wanted it himself or not; these days he's not fit to drive half the time anyway. When I got to Gorse Bank Cottage I drove the Volvo straight into the garage, jumped out and there they were, exactly as I remembered, half a dozen tools – hammer, chisel, shears and so on – lying higgle-de-piggledy on a bench and among them a saw. I picked up the saw, put it on the back seat of the car and threw a rug over it just before Stella came out of the cottage.

We had a cup of coffee together and she did her best not to be too inquisitive about Charles. I spun her a yarn about the mythical love-nest, how Charles had borrowed it from friends who were away in the Italian lakes, how it wasn't much to look at (not a patch on Gorse Bank Cottage!) but that didn't matter as I wasn't expecting to spend much time wandering round looking at the exterior anyway! . . . but don't forget, I said, if Vyvyan, or

195

anybody else, should ever come round asking questions, I got here at half past eleven and didn't leave until well after tea, we had a delicious tea together, scones and honey, remember? She laughed and crossed her heart and said don't worry, scones and honey and you didn't leave a minute before half past five . . .

I had oceans of time. I wasn't due to meet Peter Venning until half past two. And I expected him to be late. Deliberately late. Just to show me who was boss and who had to do the waiting . . . not that I minded much now . . . a man can be a bastard for so long and then, if he comes up against someone like me, he's had it . . .

I drove slowly and easily across country to Mill Race House purposely going a long way round and taking my time. I had a warm feeling of excitement inside me. Tucked away, as it were, but satisfying. I was out on my own, doing something I had planned and nobody could stop me or foul it up. It was going to be all right . . .

When I got to Mill Race House I sat in the car and ate the cold wing of chicken and the cheese biscuits I had brought from Hambledon Street. I'd brought a flask, too, with a brandy and ginger ale already mixed in it. The ginger ale had gone a bit flat, but never mind, it tasted marvellous.

Then I smoked a cigarette and kept an eye on the time. Of course that bastard Venning might come early. It was unlikely; but he might. And I didn't want to be caught out like that; I simply mustn't be caught out like that . . . so at one o'clock I got out of the car and walked up to the house.

I didn't have any of the money with me, of course. The money was still safely (well, fairly safely anyway!) hidden in the flat. Nobody was going to take that away from me. Venning had had all he was going to get, and if he thought (as I devoutly hoped he did) that there was more on the way he was in for quite a surprise.

I went on to the little wooden bridge that connected the house with one of the sheds and that spanned the mill race itself. The one on which we had been standing when he told me that he couldn't swim a stroke. The water was running as fast as ever, fairly boiling along.

The bridge was rickety ... marvellously rickety, I thought. I had brought the saw with me from the car and before I started to use it I took a long look round. I needn't have bothered. There wasn't any danger. Mill Race House stood away from the road. Screened from sight. And unless there was somebody actually on the premises I couldn't be seen by anyone.

As I knew from my previous visits there one length of the hand-rail of the bridge was in a dangerous condition already. Possibly it was dangerous enough. But I wasn't taking chances. I meant to be sure.

I started sawing through the rail close to one of the upright pieces and when I was all but through, nineteen-twentieths I suppose, I stopped.

The hand-rail was supported so precariously now that my main fear was that I had overdone things and that it would suddenly give way on its own ... it would certainly give way when anyone was pushed against it ...

I knelt down and carefully brushed the little pile of sawdust into the tumbling water below with my hands then I took the saw back to the car and hid it once more under the rug on the back seat.

Shortly after two o'clock I went up to the Mill House again and pulled down the old wooden lever that controlled the wheel.

Then I stood on the bridge (taking mighty good care not to put my hand on that splendidly treacherous rail — it would have given way at once!) and watched the wheel.

Running water is fascinating anyway. And with the wheel going round this was doubly so. Great ponderous

197

wooden paddles, turning slowly at first, then gradually faster till they were going at a great lick fairly hitting the water every time ... in that seething water and with three wooden paddles whirling round you might be the best swimmer in the world, I thought, but you wouldn't stand a chance ...

I went back to the Volvo, leant against the radiator and lit a cigarette.

When I was using my lighter my hand shook a little; but it wasn't because I was afraid. I wasn't afraid of anything. Or anybody. It was excitement.

I heard Venning's car before I expected to. He wasn't late at all, a few minutes early in fact, so it was just as well I had done everything in good time.

I watched him get out of his car. Making such a business of extricating himself. Like an old man. And paunchy when he was finally out ... you won't be doing much swimming once you're in the stream, I thought ...

'So you've turned up?' he said. I wasn't going to let his tone of voice rile me. He could be as unpleasant as he liked – for a short time ...

'Yes,' I told him, 'here I am, I've turned up.' He gave that irritating little laugh of his and said, 'You're getting sensible, Barbara; I shouldn't be surprised if you and I could get really friendly in the long run.'

I very nearly had to laugh at that because, of course, there wasn't going to be any long run.

'Where's the money?' he asked. I told him inside, and for a moment he was a bit surprised. I said I thought it was safer, nobody can see us inside. 'I don't think anyone can see us out here either,' he answered. 'Still you're probably right: can't be too careful; in we go then ...'

Just as we were coming to the little bridge (I was walking a pace or two behind him) he said the wheel's working. 'I know,' I told him, 'I turned it on; just for fun.' 'It's quite a sight, isn't it,' he said and he made the fatal mistake of stopping and leaning on the rail to have a look.

Probably he would have fallen over in any case because the way I had fixed that rail it would hardly have stood a bird perching on it. But I wasn't leaving things to chance. The moment he made to lean on the rail and look over it I shouted out something – 'go over you bastard' or something like that; I'm not sure what I did shout; I just felt like I had done when I pressed the gun against James Benson's neck and threatened to blow his head off. I felt exultant, triumphant, huge – go over you bastard I shouted and pushed him with all my strength.

He went over all right. He never stood a chance. I all but followed him myself I pushed so hard. I think I shrieked with laughter when I looked down and saw him in that boiling, buffeting stream. God, he looked funny. He was astonished and terrified and pleading. I'm sure he called out something: help, I suppose; or for God's sake; or something of that sort. Not that I heard him. There was such a ringing and thundering in my head I wouldn't have heard an earthquake.

He can't have shouted more than once anyway because in no time at all, seconds only, the water carried him under the wheel. And the wheel kept beating its great flat paddles round, fast and hard.

I stood there a little, probably for two or three minutes I should think, staring down at the water. Perhaps it was longer, perhaps it was five or ten minutes. At any rate until the red fog that was swirling about inside my head began to clear, and I started to think again.

I wasn't in the slightest bit scared; and this pleased me ... give me the knife, I thought; well I had given myself the knife, (saw, actually) and had made good use of it. I didn't think of it as murder, I thought of it as self-defence. The silly bastard had tried to interfere with what I was doing with my life and had got what was coming to him.

I walked round to the other side of the mill to where the mill race flowed out into a weedy river. I lit a cigarette and waited. I was annoyed to find how badly my hand was shaking when I used my lighter, but I got the cigarette going at last and I stood there waiting, staring at the fast-running stream.

I looked at my watch and timed things. After twenty minutes there was no sign of anything; no body, no clothes, nothing.

I was pretty certain then that the best possible result from my point of view had happened – flabby, unswimming Peter Venning had got trapped in some way under the mill wheel (perhaps been knocked out by it?) and with any luck would stay there for ever.

About his car I couldn't do anything; in time someone would find it there and begin to wonder where he was. Let them wonder I thought. I went back on to the little bridge where it had all happened and took a long, slow, careful look round. I wasn't having any Amminster gun business here. There was nothing. I had left nothing. Then I walked to the Volvo and made sure the saw was on the back seat. I got in and the engine started easily and swiftly. I took a long deep breath and smiled. I suddenly felt relaxed. Give me the knife I thought ...

'What have you been thinking about?' Vyvyan asked, looking at her curiously. 'You've been off in a sort of trance.'

Barbara laughed. 'Oh, day-dreaming. Let's go to the Lobster Pot, Vyvyan, and drink to dreams coming true. They sometimes do. Actually you can make them if you try hard enough.'

XIX

Barbara was sitting in the driving seat of the Volvo in the drive of Mill Race House. It was Wednesday, exactly a week after she had first been there with Peter Venning to look at the place.

She was smoking a cigarette, waiting for him.

So far everything (or very nearly everything) had gone according to plan.

She drew a satisfying draught of smoke down into her lungs and expelled it slowly through the open car window. She watched the miniature grey-blue cloud eddying, billowing, dispersing in the afternoon air . . .

Vyvyan had been inclined to be sticky about the car; but that didn't worry her; she could handle Vyvyan; let him go back to his Mrs Bennett, or whoever she was, and engage in some more strange conversation with that remarkable person. So the car had been all right.

And Stella Margerrison had been all right, too. Barbara had never doubted that she would be so. A woman has only got to drop a hint that she is making a fool of a man (usually of herself, too, into the bargain) and she can count on all the help she wants from her sister Eves.

'. . . *of course* I'll swear you were at the cottage all day darling if anybody asks. But who would ask anyway?'

'Nobody, I hope,' Barbara had said; and if things went right, if everything went as in careful prevision she had meticulously planned it, nobody would be asking any awkward questions.

Nearly everything had gone right.

She had made one alteration to her carefully thought-out plan.

She had not used the saw.

Thinking over her scheme (and she had thought of little else since it had first come into her head) she had come to the conclusion that a freshly sawn rail would hardly escape the notice of anyone investigating the affair.

It would be safer, she thought; to make it look as though the rickety old hand-rail had given way actually when Venning leant against it.

Immediately on arriving at Mill Race House she hurried to the little bridge and studied the hand-rail again. It was already in a dangerous condition and it took only five minutes vigorous pushing and pulling and twisting to make it just as she wanted it.

And now without any tell-tale saw-marks. Now the trap was laid.

Will you walk into my parlour ... who was fly now and who spider was triumphantly clear ...

The only thing that had gone wrong, the one thing not in her careful schedule, was that five minutes after working on the hand-rail she had suddenly been violently sick.

Out of the blue, quite unexpectedly, fright had got hold of her.

For five minutes she was terrified. The state she was in made her think of the first point-to-point in which she had ridden ... three and a half miles of fair hunting country ... a grey mare Silver Lassie, 15·2, aged ... *I shall be asking you ladies to accompany me down to the start in a few moments,* Major Lauste had said in his polite, old-fashioned way and Barbara had promptly disappeared behind the ladies' tent and been sick ...

She remembered it now vividly; but she also remembered that she had forced herself to mount Silver Lassie, had ridden the three and a half miles of fair hunting country with her heart in her mouth the entire time and had come home a triumphant first by ten lengths ...

The unexpected interlude of fear had shaken her; but

now, sitting in the Volvo, smoking to steady her nerves, she felt in command of things again.

Now she was not scared in the slightest. Excited, keyed up; but not scared.

She looked at her watch again. Venning was due and when he comes, she thought, he'll get what he deserves . . .

There was a sound at the entrance to the drive. She moistened her lips and stubbed her cigarette out in the dashboard ashtray . . .

She was ready.

The sound was wrong, somehow. And in two seconds she could see why it was wrong. It wasn't Peter Venning's nondescript old banger that came into view but a motor-cycle with a policeman riding it.

Now fear swept back again over the woman sitting in the Volvo . . . *Christ Almighty,* she thought, *what's this?* . . .

She watched while the policeman stopped his motor-cycle in the middle of the drive, pulled it up on to its stand and, removing his helmet as he walked, came towards her.

He was in his twenties, good-looking and extremely polite.

Ducking his head so that he could speak easily through the window of the Volvo he said, 'Excuse me, madam, but is there a telephone in the house?'

'I wouldn't think so,' Barbara answered. 'It's for sale.'

By this time the policeman had spotted the agent's noticeboard.

'Ah. You don't live here then?'

'No. I've just been looking over it.'

'I see.'

'Why? What's the matter?'

'There's been an accident just close to the end of the drive. There's a bad bend in the road —'

'An accident?'

'A tractor turning out of the field apparently, and according to the chap driving the tractor, though it's difficult to

203

get any sense out of him, this car came roaring round the blind bend too fast, and well – there you are!'

'Is anybody hurt?'

The policeman shot a quick look at Barbara and decided that she wasn't one to go into hysterics.

'The man's killed,' he said.

'The man on the tractor?'

'No. The man in the car – well, the whole thing is squashed up like a concertina, he never stood a chance.'

Barbara was already getting out of the Volvo.

'I wouldn't come and see if I was you, madam,' the young policeman advised kindly; but, of course, Barbara *had* to go ... *I must know,* she thought, *if it's Peter Venning I must see him there; dead; with my own eyes ...*

As soon as she got there she knew that everything was all right. The dead man wasn't pretty to look at, but she looked at him eagerly and he was Peter Venning ... the *late* Peter Venning she thought triumphantly; an unpleasant character, probably a homo; certainly a would-be blackmailer; and now finished with ...

It was the first time that Barbara had seen the aftermath of an accident close to and it wasn't pleasant.

Venning's car lay a squashed up pile of metal on the side of the road; he himself had been flung clear by some freak but in the process had suffered terrible injuries. Between his body and the car lay a wide pool of bright red blood. The tractor, in its last moment's effort to avert collision, had been slewed into the ditch. The tractor driver, a small middle-aged man, was sitting on the grassy bank holding his head in his hands, trying not to look at that bright red pool but unable to keep his eyes off it.

The young policeman was watching Barbara with some satisfaction; he had guessed she wouldn't be one to panic and he had been right.

He moved closer to her and jerked his head in the direction of the tractor driver, 'He's in a state of shock,' he said.

'He says he's only been driving the tractor a week and this lot has happened to him. He hardly knows what he's doing at the moment.'

Barbara heard without comprehending. She wasn't interested in the tractor driver.

There are some certainties which have to be underlined...

'I suppose he *is* dead?' she asked.

'That other one?' the policeman was surprised by the query itself and by the curious tone of voice in which it was asked, 'Oh Lord, yes, he's dead right enough, I'm afraid.'

Barbara, for all her inward exultation, kept a firm grip on herself ... '*I mustn't smile, she thought, I mustn't say good riddance to bad rubbish, I must just do and say nothing, look dumb ...*

She didn't do or say anything; but she didn't succeed in looking dumb ... she looked – the young policeman, studying her covertly, wasn't sure how the hell she *did* look ...

'I don't know if you can help me, madam,' he said, 'I can't leave this chap here alone with this lot and I want to get a message to the station. There's a telephone kiosk at Lytton's Cross, that's about two miles along. Would you be willing to run down there in your car and dial 999? Tell them a crash and someone killed close to Mill Race House. That will bring somebody out in no time and we can go on from there.'

'Yes, I'll do that, of course.'

'I'd be very grateful if you would, I'm sure; and I'm sorry you've been dragged into this.'

Barbara managed to restrain the urge for loud hysterical laughter which she felt rising in herself and converted it into no more than a slight and, she hoped, decorous smile.

'Well, thank goodness I'm not involved,' she said. 'A ghastly business. But if I can help in any way of course I'm only too glad to.'

When she was in the Volvo and had the engine running

the policeman asked, 'You know where Lytton's Cross is?'

'Not exactly.'

'Well, actually you've only got to keep on this road and you come to it. About two miles, I'd say. There's a post office on the left and the telephone kiosk outside. Dial 999.'

Barbara nodded.

'And thank you for your help.'

Barbara smiled.

She turned the car away from the unpleasant scene spread all over the roadway and drove off.

Very shortly the crossroads, the post office-cum-general store and the red telephone kiosk showed up just as the policeman had said they would.

For a moment or two Barbara was undecided. She was tempted to drive straight on and have nothing more to do with the affair.

But on reflection she thought this would be silly ... if she didn't dial 999 people would want to know why and might start asking questions. And she didn't want questions, although as she kept telling herself in almost incredulous disbelief there couldn't now be any danger. Peter Venning had been the only possible source of danger and Peter Venning had out-smarted himself ... no doubt he had been bowling along that winding road in joyous anticipation of having his own way, of getting all he wanted ... she gave a little harsh laugh, *well*, she thought, *in the end the bastard got more than he wanted ...*

999 she dialled in the red telephone box.

'Emergency services here. What service do you want? Police, Ambulance or Fire?'

'Police.'

'Police Emergency service here.'

'There's been a road accident close to Mill Race House. There's a man killed and one of your policemen is there on a motor-bike. He asked me to ring you.'

206

'Mill Race House. That's on the Lamington Road, isn't it?'

'I don't know.'

'Where are you speaking from?'

'I'm in a public call box. I think it's called Lytton's Cross. There's a post office here.'

'Lytton's Cross. That's it. That's on the Lamington Road. And how far away is the accident?

'Two miles.'

'Leave it to us. We'll be there. And your name, madam?'

Barbara rang off.

She drove back to London slowly, stopping once on the way in a lay-by and getting out of the car on to the grass verge because she feared she was going to be sick again . . .

Delayed shock, she thought; that pool of startlingly red blood and the tractor driver slobbering like an idiot with his head between his hands; but, of course, most and best of all the marvellous feeling of relief and release . . . if Venning had turned up at Mill Race House as she fully expected him to do she would have killed him. Everything was prepared and it would all have happened. Just as she had planned. The perfect murder. She hadn't had to do it, and the feeling of relief swept over her now and nearly made her sick again . . .

She wasn't sick and very soon the only feeling left in her was a mounting sense of triumph.

When eventually she got back to Hambledon Street Vyvyan was not yet in and she had the flat to herself.

She walked slowly through its few rooms stopping, as she did so, to note individually almost every piece of furniture, every picture . . . comfortable and civilised, she thought; and to remain comfortable and civilised you had to be ruthless . . . people got in the way; well, 'people' were out of the way now . . .

Outside the door of the glory-hole she stood for a moment, thinking. Then she fished the key out from its hiding-place and unlocked the door. She contemplated the suitcases but didn't bother to open any of them. What was in them was safe now; her insurance premium for the good life . . .

When Vyvyan came in carrying the *Evening Standard* she couldn't tell whether he had been drinking or not. Not that she cared much now . . .

She took the paper from him and began to scan it rapidly.

Eventually she discovered what she was hoping to see.

'Well, there's one good piece of news in the paper anyway, Peter Venning is dead.'

'Dead?'

'He's been killed.'

Vyvyan, turning back from the drinks table to face the room and her, looked startled.

'Did you kill him?' he asked at length.

Barbara burst out into loud laughter.

'Don't be silly. What do you think I did? Pushed him into a river or something? He crashed his car somewhere in the country and got himself killed. It says so here. And now, as you're standing there, mix me a damned good drink to celebrate it.'

XX

'So where's this red M.G. of yours with four sporting types in it, one of them a friend of Miss Beryl Carpenter?'

Detective Inspector Lawson put a certain amount of official gruffness into his query, but this was more for show than for anything else; he knew well enough that young Terence Foster had done all he could.

'The fact is, sir, I don't know. I thought I might be on to something but it has all fizzled out. I've put in a lot of work and got no joy.'

Lawson laughed.

'I wouldn't worry too much,' he said. 'You'll find that bags of hard slog and no joy is a definition of about sixty per cent of our cases.'

'I suppose so, sir.'

'You can take it from me as a fact.'

'If we could have traced that car we could have found the girl who went as an au pair to the Bensons.'

'Cheer up, we might still find her.'

It was a morale boosting sentence in which the inspector himself no longer had much real belief; the Amminster bank robbery still nagged uncomfortably at him but by now it had definitely been relegated to the back of his mind. Other matters had come crowding in day by day and had demanded immediate attention; he was slowly beginning to think that he would have to accept the view that the once-only villains who had pulled off the Amminster job had got away with it.

Just to prove how wrong he was within half an hour of Foster's exit from the office the sergeant came in. There were routine matters that had to be dealt with; forms to be filled up; certificates to be signed.

'I might as well remuster as a ruddy clerk and have done with it,' Lawson grumbled.

The sergeant chuckled sympathetically, 'That's the lot, sir,' he said picking up the last signed paper. 'You can go back to being a brutal policeman now and give these Civil Liberty people something to howl about. God, what a bunch.'

'We've got to put up with all sorts in our job,' the inspector said philosophically.

'I suppose so. But when that lot start bleating about liberty I must admit it gets up my nose a bit. One of them kicks a policeman in the face and it's a brave blow for democracy, the policeman catches hold of the thug's foot to ward off the kick and it's brutality, headlined in the left-wing press and highlighted on television. Liberty! if ever that gang get in charge we'll all be at liberty to do exactly what they tell us and quick about it, or else; à la Ruskies.'

It had been a long day and Lawson was anxious to get home, not to prolong conversation in the office.

'That's the lot then?' he inquired.

'That's it, sir.' The sergeant was on his way out, at the door he turned.

'By the way; the Amminster bank case; weren't you interested in a chap called Venning, an antique dealer?'

Lawson was already getting his coat down off its peg; he turned quickly.

'Yes, I was. Why?'

'He's killed himself in a motor smash.'

'He has?'

'It's in the evening paper. I saw it just before coming in to you.'

'An accident? Anybody with him? Anybody else involved?'

'It doesn't say anything about a passenger. The other half of the accident was a tractor apparently. A chap coming out on to the road through a field gate at an awkward turn.'

'Was he injured?'

'No. Shaken up and taken to hospital for a check, then sent home seemingly.'

'Where was this?'

'Sussex. Haywards Heath area.'

'What was Venning doing down there?'

The sergeant laughed. 'Well, I don't know that, sir, do I? I suppose he could have been doing half a dozen things.'

'Yes, of course he could. All right. Thank you.'

After the business of putting on his coat and arranging his scarf ... the sergeant was right, of course, antique dealer Venning could have been on half a dozen different ploys, all of them perfectly legal. But a man doesn't give up hunches easily. Certainly Detective Inspector William Lawson didn't. Ever since he had first visited Tooveys antique shop and made the acquaintance of its proprietor his hunch had been that there was a scent there waiting to be picked up if only he could once get on to it.

He didn't really have much hope of anything coming from it, but now, already coated and scarved, he sat down again at his desk and reached for the telephone ...

'As far as we can see just a straightforward accident,' Haywards Heath told him obligingly. 'This chap was coming out of the field on the tractor; actually it was his first day driving the thing and my guess is he wasn't completely at ease on it. Of course the road *is* dangerous there, no doubt about it, it's narrow and there's a long bend and anyone in their senses would think thirty plenty fast enough. According to the chap on the tractor the car came round the bend like a bat out of hell, but there weren't any witnesses so what can you do?'

'There was nobody in the car with Venning?'

'No. No passengers.'

'And he was killed outright?'

'Must have been. Can't have stood a chance. So our man

said. By sheer chance one of our m/c patrols came along the road just after the crash occurred. When he got on the scene there was a lot of arterial blood about; the driver of the car was dead; and the tractor man was in such a state he was practically gibbering.'

'You've no idea why Venning was there of course?'

'Why he was there? No. None. How could we have? Why, are you interested in him?'

'Could be. What happened after the crash?'

'The first thing we knew was this woman dialling 999.'

'What woman?'

'The accident occurred close to the end of a side road, more or less a private drive apparently leading up to a place called Mill Race House. So our patrol man went up to see if there was a telephone there. He was unlucky about the telephone because the house is empty and up for sale, but there was a woman sitting in a car in front of it.

'She had come down to have a look round, I suppose with an idea of buying. She hadn't seen the accident and in fact had nothing to do with it so she was no good as a witness, but she certainly turned out helpful.

'P.C. Jenks, that's our patrol man, thought he ought to stay on the scene because of the body there and also because the tractor driver was close to a state of collapse so he asked this woman would she mind going in her Volvo two miles down the road to a place called Lytton's Cross where there was a telephone box —'

'Going in her *what?*' the inspector asked quietly.

'Her Volvo. Her car.'

'This woman was driving a Volvo?'

'Yes. Interested?'

'Did P.C. Jenks get her name?'

'No, he didn't.'

'Pity.'

'Jenks is a good man. One of our best. But this woman had absolutely nothing to do with the accident. She wasn't concerned in it. She hadn't even seen it. All he wanted her to do was to get a message to the emergency services. Which she did.'

'No one has seen her since I suppose?'

'No. But, like I say, Jenks is a good man. He's got his head screwed on right. As she was driving away in her Volvo towards Lytton's Cross it struck him that it might have been wiser to ask for her name and address so just before the Volvo disappeared round the curve of the road he whipped out his notebook and took down the registration number.'

'Oh, good for Jenks,' Lawson said. 'Good for Jenks. Make him up to sergeant when you get a chance. What's the number?'

There was a pause, but not a very long one, then Haywards Heath said UCD 196 J.

Detective Inspector Lawson wrote it down.

'Well, I think that's about all we can tell you,' Haywards Heath said cheerfully.

'Thanks a lot,' the inspector answered. 'I'll see what I can do with it.'

It takes only a little time to trace an individual car to its current owner when you are in possession of the registration number. Detective Inspector William Lawson did it without any real difficulty and with the minimum of delay.

Four hours after being in possession of the knowledge he was on his way along the King's Road. He was too busy a person to get to London often, and in any case too provincial a man even to want to do so; and his walk down the King's Road, Chelsea, made him think that he hadn't been missing much.

He came to the corner of Hambledon Street and turned along it. The street which fifty years ago must have been an agreeable little living area now looked like a large open-air garage; cars were parked on both sides of it, most of them spreading half their width across the narrow pavement.

213

A large printed notice dealing with the question of local parking was affixed to a lamp-post. Lawson stopped to read it; and was glad he had done so. The Volvo lead was a tenuous one and acting on his customary principle of 'Softlee softlee catchee monkey' the inspector was very anxious at this early stage not to give anyone cause for alarm. The notice about the local battle about parking had given him an idea.

Halfway along the street on the left-hand side he saw the Volvo UDC 196 J standing like all its fellows half in the roadway, half on the pavement.

When he saw it he felt a slight stir of excitement. Wild goose chase or at last the crack in the case? Impossible to tell. Foolish to be optimistic about it as he well knew, but at least he was on some sort of trail again . . .

Even if the name and address had not been written in a notebook in one of the pockets of his somewhat nondescript tweed jacket they were firmly fixed in his head.

He saw the appropriately marked (Weighman) bellpush outside the front door and pressed it.

After a delay long enough to make Lawson contemplate ringing again the door was opened by a man.

The inspector, used to quick assessments, took stock of him . . . public-school type; fortyish, could be bad tempered if he wanted, letting himself go to seed a bit, too many double gins probably – was his two seconds summing up.

'Mr Weighman?' he asked politely.

'What is it?'

'This parking business, Mr Weighman —'

'For God's sake what's wrong now? Usually the street's full up with cars from other districts and people living here can't get near the place. What am I doing wrong *now* for Pete's sake?'

Lawson smiled reassuringly.

'Absolutely nothing wrong, Mr Weighman. It's nothing

like that. The Council are thinking of bringing Hambledon Street into the Residents' Parking Scheme and so make it easier for the people living here.'

'About time too. You're from the Council presumably. I'd just like you to tell me why the hell your lot haven't got round to this before.'

'Personally I'm all for it, Mr Weighman; but before the Council can do anything they've got to know the feelings of residents on the question. That's why I'm coming round explaining the scheme and asking for people's views.'

'Come inside for five minutes and I'll let you know what I think about it,' Vyvyan said.

Inside Lawson saw that it wasn't double gins but double whiskies that were the cause of the trouble. He was offered one immediately and made the appropriate reply, 'Well, it's very kind of you, Mr Weighman, I don't mind if I do —'

His host obviously didn't mind if *he* did either.

'I ought to give this stuff up really,' he said, handing a generously charged glass to Lawson, 'or so people tell me.'

'Ah, the things people tell us!'

'But, when you come to think of it, what's the point in giving anything up?'

'What indeed, sir. Good health.'

'I'll tell you about the parking problem in this street,' Vyvyan said 'and then you can go back to the Town Hall, or wherever it is you come from, and maybe be able to persuade the half-blind idiots there to do something sensible about it —'

Lawson listened with apparently close attention to a five minute harangue about the stupidity of local officials and the hardships of the average motorist.

Being a motorist himself he thought there was a good deal of sense in what was said, but the parking problems of the residents of Hambledon Street were not really occupying his mind much; while his host was talking the inspector was busy with his eyes . . .

215

'Well, there you are,' Vyvyan ended up, 'that's my view of it anyway. Maybe you can do something about it.'

'I'll certainly try, sir,' Lawson said rising to his feet, 'Oh – I'm sorry.'

In rising he had clumsily upset a small circular occasional table standing close by his chair. An ashtray and two books that had been resting on it were sent crashing on to the floor.

Vyvyan stooped to retrieve them while Lawson was still apologising . . .

Shortly after ten o'clock the following morning the inspector brought his car to a halt outside 'Wenlock'. Mrs Benson herself came to the door to answer his ring and was at first reluctant to ask him in.

Once inside the reason was apparent: 'Wenlock', once the cosiest of little conventional provincial love nests was in disorder.

'We're moving,' Muriel Benson explained, not far from tears.

'Moving?'

'We've got to. Arthur has been retired by the bank because of that awful robbery business and we can't go on living here. Of course he let that girl make a fool of him; I realise that. So does he now. But then she made fools of both of us if it comes to that. My word, I wish you could catch her, Inspector.'

'Is that what she looked like?' he asked.

'Yes, that's her. Wherever did you get that photograph from?'

The inspector didn't bother to explain that he had swiped the photograph off a desk in the living-room of a flat in Hambledon Street Chelsea while his host was busy retrieving some fallen objects from the floor.

'You're sure that woman is the one who called herself

Beryl Carpenter?' he asked.

'Of course I'm sure. That's Beryl Carpenter all right. You've found her, then?'

'Not yet. Not quite. But I'm on the way.'

XXI

Barbara got out of the green, pine-scented hot water and stood naked on the bathroom scales.

She was pleased by what the pointer told her. She certainly hadn't put on any weight and by shifting her stance slightly it was possible to give herself reason for thinking that she had even lost a fraction.

She stepped off the scales and, still naked, opened the door and called across the minute hall into the living-room.

'Vyvyan.'

Vyvyan duly appeared as summoned.

'Have you any champers left?'

'A bottle or two.'

'Let's kill one. I feel like celebrating.'

'Celebrating what?'

'That bastard Venning being out of our way.'

Ten minutes later, now clad in a long yellow house-coat and wearing nothing whatever underneath it, she came into the living-room and took up her favourite seat on the low stool in front of the fire.

The room pleased her as it always did when she examined it critically. Tonight she found it doubly pleasing; she was feeling on top of the world.

Vyvyan was in the corner by the drinks table dealing with a recalcitrant cork ... she considered him; and in considering him considered, as she was well aware, herself ... the man she had chosen to live with ... at the moment getting rather red in the face from his efforts with the champagne cork ... selfish, passionate, a-moral ... *just like me*, she thought ... something *to* him, tho', when you could keep him off the bottle – *if* you could keep him off the

bottle, if ultimately you *wanted* to keep him off the bottle
... *my sort really, I suppose; birds of a feather* ... there
might be something to be said for legalising the whole position and marrying the man ... easy to laugh at the business
of marriage, middle-class superstition, monstrous arrogance
of the clergy and so on and so on; impossible to deny however that the out-worn, out-dated, discredited institution
did, somehow, have something about it, especially for a
woman ... Of course there was Charles to be considered
... Charles had been getting more infatuated of late; something to do with his age perhaps ... she was having lots of
fun with Charles and it probably wouldn't be difficult, by a
judicious withholding of favours, to bring him to the point
of idiocy which would mean the tiresome drawn out
tediousness of divorce and ultimately all the 'duchess' and
'Your Grace' business ... there had been moments during
the past weeks when Barbara had found this prospect
tempting ... in some ways it still was ... but with 'duchess'
and 'Your Grace' would come too, a whole way of life – she
could see the tedious duties and functions stretching end-
lessly ahead – which for nine-tenths of the time she knew
she would find unutterably boring ... and middle-aged
dukes who got rid of their duchesses had a way of repeating
the performance before many years were up; there was always that to consider ... the man who had at that precise
moment succeeded in opening the bottle of champagne at
the far end of the room was more in her line ... awkward,
bad-tempered, moody, even *odd* at times (all that Mrs
Bennett business!) but *her sort* ... No need to jettison
Charles completely, of course: Vyvyan, whom she was now
used to, as a complaisant background, possibly even as a
husband; the warm, small, civilised flat in Hambledon
Street as a comfortable base; ducal Charles in the offing as
an occasional diversion; an interesting and in time lucrative
job with Stella Margerrison, *and now no more worries*
about money; what more could a girl ask she thought ...

'I hope it's cold enough,' Vyvyan said bringing her glass to her.

'You ought to stick to this and drop the hard stuff.'

'Thanks for the advice.'

She looked at him over the top of her brimming glass, 'You and that Mrs Bennett of yours,' she said with a kind of affectionate contempt.

Vyvyan sipped his drink and set down his glass. He seemed to be considering Barbara's words. Eventually he said, 'Mrs Bennett is a remarkable person.'

'I'm sure she is.'

'I don't think you're sure of anything of the kind. All you're sure about, all you care about, is yourself. You're that sort.'

Not a whit put out Barbara laughed. 'Quite right, I am. So are you. Up us and to hell with everybody else. That's why we get on together. You do agree that we get on together, don't you?'

'Oh yes, we get on together.'

'We might even consider making it permanent. Why not? We can't help being partners now. After all you thought up the perfect crime and I helped you carry it out – I did help you, didn't I?'

'You certainly did.'

'O.K., then. Partners. And now Peter Venning's out of the way we're quids in. Let's drink to it,' she raised her glass and as she was doing so the doorbell rang.

'Who the hell's that?' she said. 'Whoever it is, get rid of them quickly. I don't think we shall be wanting visitors for a bit shall we?'

At the door Vyvyan recognised his caller.

'Damn it, not about the parking scheme again, surely,' he said.

'No. Not about the parking this time, Mr Weighman.'

'What then?'

Detective Inspector Lawson produced his identity card

and said quietly, 'I am a police officer and I am investigating a robbery from Barrolds bank in Amminster on Friday April the twenty-third last. I have reason to believe that you and a woman living in this house with you can help me in my inquiries.'

Vyvyan answered nothing at all. Impelled possibly only by curiosity, but possibly by some much more deeply seated prompting, Barbara opened the living-room door and spoke into the hall.

'What's going on?' she asked. 'Who are you?'

The inspector smiled when he saw her.

'It's rather a question of who you are,' he answered. 'For a number of weeks Mrs James Benson of "Wenlock", Amminster, thought you were Miss Beryl Carpenter, I believe . . .'